Praise for Why Did I Ever

"[Robison] finds the exact place where language and existence intersect ... Her un-self-conscious oddballs, her eye for the curious detail, the way she uses tiny circles of logic to create a worldview—all of Robison's minimalist genius is at work here."
—Cathleen Schine, *The New York Times Book Review*

"[T]here's a grace and humor in the slippage between the ideal and the real ... [Robison] here creates a narrative out of fragmented paragraphs, and the book works best when she strips Money's most explicit fears away. At these moments, a simple sentence fragment ... seems as close to a perfect expression of lost beauty."
—*The New Yorker*

"Mary Robison, almost as an afterthought, has created a novel that speaks volumes about life in Los Angeles: its stopping and starting, its rushing and emoting, its whimsy and its suspicious, subversive humor ... "
—*Los Angeles Times Book Review*

"Mary Robison is, and always has been, a wonderful writer. *Why Did I Ever* is startling, deft, extremely attractive, and smart—very smart—in its midnight vision of the lived life."
—Richard Ford

"Mary Robison has done for the Hollywood culture of our time what Joan Didion did thirty years ago. Spare and ruthless, precisely chiseled, *Why Did I Ever* is the *Play It As It Lays* of the twenty-first century."
—Madison Smartt Bell

"Mary Robison's stunned and plunging characters are the truth. This is pure, grim poetry."
—Barry Hannah

"Tense, moving, and hilarious ... Reading [this] dark jewel of a novel is like looking through a kaleidoscope that fractures reality—and magically, in the process, manages to convey a clearer view of the world than the seemingly more representative vision we can see with our naked eye."
—Francine Prose, *O, The Oprah Magazine*

"[A] tour de force of minimalist yet mind-expanding prose ... [Robison] makes you think—hard—about life's unavoidable travails, while making it impossible for you to suppress a smile."
—Lisa Shea, *Elle*

"What makes Money memorable, and Mary Robison essential, is that her fundamental bearings are the right ones. Love and compassion are her nature, and they suffuse the page whenever she is talking about her children, even the exasperating daughter."
—Richard Dyer, *Boston Globe*

Why Did I Ever

Why Did I Ever

MARY ROBISON

COUNTERPOINT
WASHINGTON, D.C.
NEW YORK, N.Y.

for my daughters,

my sisters,

my mother,

and for Gray

Library of Congress Cataloging-in-Publication Data
Robison, Mary.
Why did I ever / Mary Robison.
p. cm.
ISBN 1-58243-255-4 (alk. paper)
1. Middle aged women—Fiction. I. Title
PS3568.O317 W49 2001
813'.54—dc21   2001032326

Book design and composition by Mark McGarry,
Texas Type & Book Works Inc.
Set in Stempel Garamond

COUNTERPOINT
387 Park Avenue South
New York, NY 10016-8810

Counterpoint is a member of the Perseus Books Group

Printed in the United States of America on acid-free paper
that meets the American National Standards Institute z39-48 standard

10 9 8 7 6 5 4 3 2 1

Chapter One

1

I have a dream of working a combination lock that is engraved on its back with the combination. Left 85, right 12, left 66. "Well *shit,* man," I say in the dream.

2

Hollis and I have killed this whole Saturday together. We've watched all fourteen hours of the PBS series *The Civil War.*

Now that it's over he turns to me and says, "That was good."

Buy Me Something

I end up at Appletree—the grocery—in the dead of the night. I'm not going to last long shopping, though, because this song was bad enough when what's-her-name sang it. And who are all these people at four A.M.? I'm making a new rule: No one is to touch me. Unless and until I feel different about things. Then, I'll call off the rule.

4

Three ex-husbands or whoever they were.

I'm sure they have their opinions.

I would say to them, "Peace, our timing was bad, the light was ugly, things didn't work out." I'd say, "Although you certainly were doing your all, now weren't you."

I would say, "Drink!"

5

Hollis is not my ex-anything and not my boyfriend. He's my friend. Maybe not the best friend I have in the world. He is, however, the only.

6

Daughter Mev confides in me. She says that at the Methadone clinic whenever a urine sample is required, she presents a sample of the soft drink Mellow Yellow.

"You won't get caught," I tell her.

She says, "Some folks hand over Mountain Dew."

"They won't get caught either," I say. "Not to worry."

"If they think you're hoarding your dose, though," says Mev. "You know, like you're going to save it and spit it into your thing? Because who wants to go to the clinic every day?

You could never do drugs! If they think that, they go, 'Say good-bye, Mev.' And they make you say good-bye."

7

Nowadays, I don't try to talk. I try to do the talking. So I don't talk. Or, at least, I try not to.

8

Here I have retrieved from beneath the refrigerator these thirty or forty fur-covered toy mice. These cost me hundreds of dollars over the years and have a street value of many hundreds of dollars. So why doesn't the cat—lying on her side there with her eyes squeezed shut—show any appreciation?

9

I'm sitting alone in my vehicle, on the street before my place. It's only just after dawn, yet here's Hollis, strolling up, munching from a box of Cracker Jacks.

He stoops at my window and says to me, "uh oh, I hear Marianne Faithful." He straightens, shakes his Cracker Jacks box empty, scrunches it, and lobs it into the side yard. The shirt Hollis is wearing has a pattern of skylarks, I believe they are, depicted on it.

He plants a hand on the car now and drums his fingers. He stoops again and says, "I've been reading an interesting book on John Wayne. You are what, here? Feeling neglected?"

"No," I say, turning to look at him. "No. Nor do I feel hungry for apples, Hollis." I say, "Those are two among the feelings I do not have."

10

The name I use is an annoying problem. Everyone wonders about it. No one doesn't ask.

My name is Money. I picked it up and kept it and now it's what I'm called.

I say I'm tired of telling how I got the name. Or that the story isn't all that great.

Still Something Missing

"I need plywood," said my son, Paulie, in his sleep. Or I heard wrong. I know it was "need" something.

That was my first day there, at his flat on St. Anne, before NYPD began hiding him.

He looked like this: in white cotton socks and frayed blue jeans, a cowhide belt and a petal-green sweater. His hands in their horrible bandage gloves must've been on his lap and I couldn't see them because he was bent over, with his plate pushed aside and his face on the dining table, and he was all-the-way asleep, with a tiny chip of emerald glinting there in the lobe of his ear.

12

Days went by and he still kept ignoring all the stuff I'd brought for him. Fine stuff, but Paulie couldn't get in the mood. And he was in something like pain when I finally set each thing out and presented it as though it were for sale. *What*, could've been wrong with me? Handkerchiefs! I told him about the quality. "Just wait'll you go to use one of these." He was three weeks out of the hospital. I should have ground the things up into bits and shreds in the garbage disposal.

A World of Love

I'm a script doctor, as far as I know this afternoon at three o'clock central time. And I'm due back at the studio according to Belinda who's the development producer or whatever is her job.

She has some hair shirt or other laid out for me.

Belinda is not warm. She's small-minded, mean, picky-petty.

Someday I will learn kickboxing and I will show up at Mercury Brothers and kickbox the *stuffings* out of her.

14

For my living room I have forged three paintings and signed them all "Robert Motherwell." The paintings aren't that successful really as I went too fast. They might fool a rich fellow who doesn't expect to see a fake if anyone like that ever comes over here.

I was spurred further to autograph and personally inscribe all my books. My handwriting in them experiences a change or two and can seem manly or decorative or as if I were rushed.

The inscription in Thomas Mann's *Buddenbrooks* reads: "Party girl. Bring back my VCR."

I'm fairly proud of the Rothko I forged for my bedroom. Whereas the blacks in the paintings at the Rothko Chapel can look a little steely and cold, my blacks are rich with the colors of hot embers and dark earth.

15

"Now my throat hurts from screaming at you!" I tell Hollis.

We're in my bedroom, standing *before* the Rothko, with our feet planted wide apart and our arms crossed.

"What's missing here is a focal point," he says. "Something for our eyes to fix on, finally, and rest upon. Something we end up gazing at."

"It's! A! Copy!" I shriek at him.

16

Something else that makes me angry is that I got too old to prostitute myself. I wasn't going to anyway but it was there, it was my Z plan.

17

Nine West, I've never really had great luck with their shoes. They can look terrific but they have sharp arches and hard fucking soles.

Once in New York on my way to Penn Station I had to stop and remove the Nine West shoes I was wearing. I had to walk on in my stocking feet. Barrabus, I think he was called, was with me. My husband then but he wouldn't wait up, wouldn't take an extra minute out, oh no.

"Just keep going!" I called to him. "However eventually, I will meet you there."

That ex I heard was arrested for stealing food. Maybe I only dreamed it. It's what I tell people, anyway.

18

I call my doctor's office to ask for some Ritalin. His nurse answers and says, "This is Annabelle. According to our records, you're not due for a prescription at this time."

I say, "Annabelle, this is not what it appears."

"Oh?" she says and waits because she was trained to wait and force me to do the synopsizing.

I will take that challenge. "There was a series of mishaps," I tell her. "Some were spilled at the sink or ruined by moisture. Then a vial I use for travel got mislaid and they're gone. I'm out," I say. "Who can explain it?"

But I'm a stupid woman for asking that question. Nurse Annabelle can explain what happened to my drugs.

Without Ritalin I can sustain an evil thought or two, such as: "That there feels like cancer of the esophagus." However, I'm liable to skip over more routine kinds of thinking, such as, "Move up in line here," or "Steer."

So I'm in bed. I'm in bed unless Dr. Rex himself calls to inform me he's written new prescriptions.

More emphatically, I am in bed until.

19

I notice on the news when they're interviewing people, there's an attractive man in Chicago. His name goes by too fast but I'd know the guy if I saw him again.

Empty Your Pockets

I hate Bell South and so raise my voice and warn their representatives that I will take my business elsewhere.

I mention this to Hollis and tell him of the many new friends I have made—others who were present in the Bell South office, customers who overheard my threat. These are the same people who feel shamefaced, I explain, for falling behind in their phone service payments.

"Well . . .," Hollis begins. Ah, but I have my eye on him.

21

Now he and I are watching some men with a ball. No matter the shape or size of the ball, what team or for what country the men fight. The TV is showing men with a ball so we're watching.

22

"In my head," I tell him, "are the works of John Philip Sousa. And so loud that at first I thought the high school's band was practicing. I went and checked outside. I don't even know the words to 'It's a Grand Old Flag.'"

"Oh, come on," says he. "'It's a grand old flag, dunt dunt high-flying flag. Dunt dunt duh, dunt dunt duh, dunt dunt duhhh.'"

23

There are real and scary sounds from outside my place. They are like a woman running.

While I have the door opened an inch, trying to see what's what, Flower Girl my cat skitters out.

And now the running woman is gone.

I call 911 but hang up when the operator asks whether I'm phoning from a home or a residence.

There's disorder out there under the traffic light. At the intersection, a bread truck has been tipped up onto its nose and then—it would seem—hammered.

Hollis crowds me for a view through the window.

I say to him, "See that girl behind everything? In the pink midi-top?"

I say, "Suppose you were standing next to that girl. You wouldn't reach out and grab her breasts, now would you?"

He takes a drink from his bottle of red vegetable juice. Wags his head, no.

"You'd behave decently toward her and uphold your own personal standards, correct?"

His head moves, yes.

I say, "O.K., then let's start all over at the beginning. Because I still really believe in my heart that men can be educated."

"That's a Roman Meal bread truck," he says, "that got hit. You want me to go see if I can snick us a couple of loaves?"

I Should Be Going

I take a lengthy drive in case there's some music I want to buy.

I drive to Montgomery, Alabama—thousands of miles from my home. It's three or four or five in the morning. All that's open here is a Wal-Mart and the very best music they're selling is an old Michael Jackson single, "Blood on the Dance Floor."

Which, it turns out, isn't so bad. Especially if you eliminate the treble.

The police think it's bad. Their patrol car slows as they ride alongside me. They shine a light, bark a warning. I click the sound down. They surge ahead. I switch the sound up loud again. The patrol car slows, same flashlight, same warning.

I'm tempted but I dissuade myself from going through it all a third time. My excuses are just excuses and they are not good enough.

25

I get lost driving back and do the same exits and merges for hours and hours. I wonder if an aerial view of me might be fun to watch.

And now I've made an error and there are eighteen-wheelers stopped ahead of me, eighteen-wheelers behind. And not for a great long while will I be released from the lineup for this weigh station.

Could Stand Here for Hours

"You need more than just the bangs cut," says the hair stylist. "You look like Cochise."

And I see in the restroom mirror as I'm drawing on lipstick that I don't want my mouth. I say, "Don't ever use a straw again. Don't whistle. Or whisper. Or say 'What,' or 'Who.'"

27

I do know some horrible stories. One story about my son may never have an end to it. Or the story will have an end I don't want to know because it's horrible. Want to or not, I have to wait, wait, wait.

28

Both my kids have flame-glo hair and turquoise eyes. One summer after they had earned all their college degrees, they found work doing the cake displays in a bakery and we had sweets to eat. That was in D.C. or someplace we lived then.

Mev went on to a job carving wooden forks and spoons. Paulie moved to New York and, I believe, checked skates at the counter in Roller World.

29

Here now is Mev, on the walkway, her face fired green from the sun through the trees. She's standing lopsided, with her arms raised unevenly in question. She asks, "How is it that with red Rit dye, the stuff always comes out that Krishna color?"

"I'm to blame for that," I say. "It's because you're your mother's daughter."

"Wow," she says and sits down with me on the concrete bench.

I say, "Everybody else gets red."

30

The thing about Mev is she has twice failed the bar exam.

"You can fail it a *third* time, though, can't you?" Hollis asks her.

Mev says, "No, see, at this point, even to do that, I'd have to brush up and study."

31

In Appletree, she says, "There's my friend Margaret, over at the orange juice."

"Who?"

"My friend Margaret that lives near me on Southy. I got that angora sweater from her? The one who does the bookmobile. I waved but I guess she doesn't see me."

I'm looking. I say, "The only person anywhere near the orange juice is ninety-two years old."

"What about it, Mother?"

"Nothing," I say. "Nothing about it at all."

Mev always finds friends and they're always older. They're people who were born at home.

32

She makes herself a part of things—over in the smoke niche fetching Lucky Strikes for that man, now dragging somebody's Moderow baby crib up to the cashier. Her brother's the same way. I boarded a subway with him once and he went along the car like a porter, seating people and catching parcels before they spilled.

And It's Just My Size

Hollis reads to me from a dictionary: "'Oscillate...A vibrating motion as things move backward and forward, vary or vacillate between differing conditions and become stronger and weaker.'"

"Huh," I say. "Well, but that describes me."

34

"Can I just say something?" he asks, and he starts to. So I remind him that permission to say something is not permission to say anything.

Therefore, he decides to write down for me in longhand what it is that he has to say. Or, he would like to. He attempts to. First he must test his pen for ink.

I vacate the room without ever learning if his letter-writing effort is successful.

All We Do Is Argue

"I know what you're thinking," I say to myself.

"O.K.," I say, "*What?*"

"It's that thing in your hand. You're thinking that it goes someplace."

"Then where does it go?" I ask.

"Well, not up there...," I say as I'm climbing the stairs.

"So important to you to be right," I say, climbing back down.

36

Martin, some person I know, has compiled a list of the five hundred best rock singles ever recorded. Number 11 on the list is "Sunny Afternoon" by the Kinks. Or if it's not number 11, it should be.

You Decide

Things break. I head for the hardware.

I have to walk past my neighbor who's forever out on the bench here in our yard. The Deaf Lady. She isn't deaf; a little bit, not very. She won't tell me why she's called that. She'll say, "I'd rather not go into it," or, "I'd prefer you weren't involved."

The light out here is weird, the day already fading. The Deaf Lady looks as if she can't locate her doll. "What's the matter?" I ask her.

"Just mistakes I make," she says. "Like I left the kitchen thing burning again. On the what's-it-called? Not the dashboard."

"The oven top. Coil stove. The *burners*," I say. "But everybody does that. How long did you leave it on?"

"Since the other night, I guess, when I was making fudge."

I scoot her over so I can sit down. "Well, it's happened to me," I say. "Never for days on end, that I recall."

"You want to go somewhere and eat?" she asks.

"Sure."

"O.K., good," she says. "Where do you want to go?"

"Oh, I don't care. It doesn't matter. Anyplace is fine."

She says, "Then let's just go to the city dump and eat rats! All we have to do is catch them."

38

We end up at the River Cafe on Science Street. Who works here according to their name tags are Toadstool and Paranoid Phil.

My Asparagus Tips Casserole has no asparagus.

"How're you doing?" the two servers ask me.

They must mean with this food.

"You guys are spoiling me," I say.

Across from us is the cashier's counter. There, a girl in a black T-shirt stenciled with the word "Jezebel" is wagging her head at a woman in a muumuu who's sadly, slowly, reluctantly writing a check. Now a squat fellow appears outside the place and squints at the door menu. He wanders off, comes back, reads the menu some more, wanders off.

Lollipops Are Only for the Kids Who Had Shots

Most of the movie studios have fired me. The William Morris Agency just fired me. Two of their agents on a conference line regretted that maybe they've been holding me back. They've fired me so they won't hold me back anymore.

Now I couldn't be happier because here's what I get to do: Run the bathroom tap water until it's really cold, plug the tub up and fill it to the brim, and then *into* the chilly water plunge the Umani Fax Machine, the Sukosonic modem, the 1309 Phone Mail System, the beeper.

"Good-bye. Go to hell," I say to them.

Mercury Brothers is about the only studio I have left. Mercury Brothers and their producer witch, Belinda.

There Is No They

"It'll never change," Hollis says, beside me in the car. "No matter how long we sit here, it'll still be a stop sign."

Hollis is a Driver's Ed. instructor. I say, "So this is what it must be like to study under you."

He sips noisily to the end of his lime drink, now sends the jumbo paper cup flying from the car window.

He is just coming up with shit. He says, "At least I made you stop dyeing your hair. That purple shoeshine color or what was it? Remember?"

"No," I say. "And I believe I would."

42

I would say to this or that ex: "Maybe I didn't understand you or pay enough attention. There was a little bridge or something I failed to cross over. It was on the day you helped me wax the hallway and the little stairs, when you said to me, 'The floor will be dry in a minute.' Between the time you said that and when you asked me, 'Do *you* think my pubic hair's such an unusual color?'"

And Another Thing

I have now done Blockbuster. *Little Dorrit*, Parts One and Two.

44

I'm pressed up against a telephone pole, nailing it with a poster of my missing cat.

Now I'm bustling off, for I've noticed the Ichabod landlord working in the bushes. He strictly does not allow pets.

Now I'm at the next pole making a loud production of nailing Flower Girl's poster because I know right from wrong and my dealings with the landlord are less important than the swift return of my cat.

45

Through the window is a lavender sky and a red orb of sun and the Deaf Lady out there with a half-filled air balloon. She's staring ahead, her cheeks flushed, her eyes intense, readying herself to pump up the rest of it.

Inside here is Hollis, and the clock, and the "wick-wick" of the ceiling fan, and the television left going out on the sun porch, transmitting the voice of Paul Newman in *Hud*.

"Hollis," I say. "On that thing we were discussing. What are my other choices?"

He blows a smoke ring into the reach of the fan. "No others," he says. "You don't get any more."

I gaze at the fireplace, at its yellow-tiled face, at the mantel, with its huddle of red votive candles.

He can never just answer me. If I ask, "How're you doing?" he asks, "Compared to whom?" I ask, "May I tell you something?" and he says, "Still America." That is what I have to put up with, day, after day, after day.

Chapter Two

Life in the Car

I drive all over the American South, all night long, and nobody gives me trouble.

Maybe this farmer would but I buzz down my window and scream at him, "Remember *Goat's Head Soup?* What an album! To my mind, it is worth hearing again!"

Couples, in the cars on this interstate, I think, "Ugh. They are stuck." I think the women must envy me, driving a hundred and five with nobody saying not to, barefoot and chain-smoking and squawking along to a song.

And Yet

Overconfidence is a mistake for me. Not a big one, but it kicks open the door for several others.

49

Now I don't care about sitting up straight and I'm going to break speed records in Alabama.

Or no I am not, because the U.S. Army is in front of me. You would think that the Army would drive very fast. Not so, at least not in peace time. Good, one more reason to hate the Army. They're holding me up.

50

Here's a sign that reads: "PORK!" Some signs aren't there to make you happy.

51

In sleepiness, I see a rabble of dogs in a steamy heath, their hard-featured faces mottled with light from the yellow moon. I wonder if my cat's sleeping somewhere, if she's dreaming.

There could be nothing worse than wondering about my son Paulie's dreams.

52

"WORK FOR US" reads the purple neon writing over a trucker's garage.

I say, "Thanks, but I just want to drive right now."

53

Paulie's hands. They're large to begin with, and make him bashful and can sometimes seem in his way. Now he has, in reaction to some goop he's taking, a rash and must wear white gloves. Big ridiculous gloves. So it's even more like he's in a cartoon.

Turn off the Radio

There are alcoholics all over the South. Many of them are inside the cars on this same highway. The alcoholics left over are minding the store.

55

My wheel explodes as I'm ripping past Mobile. The drunk road workers left a concrete chunk of debris out for me, smack-dab in the center of the interstate.

But I shouldn't talk. I'm just one more thigamabob.

Waiting around.

And there are two capital letters on my gearshift panel that I can't identify. I've never had to go down there.

56

Maybe I should be dead sixteen ways, but they can sledgehammer my rim back into shape and plug on any old tire; I'll pay. Because these folks are fine at the wheel replacement facility. They're no different. They're practically the same as the same people I meet over and over in the middle of the night in Mobile when something very frightening is happening to me.

We're congregated in a stifling hut—the stucco mechanics' garage.

I lean on a tiled wall. There are fizzing snapping light tubes overhead. The room seems hollowed out to me, a green cavity.

I try to talk to them. I say, "Did you ever read *Pierre; or, The Ambiguities?* It's the most disturbing Melville."

I am crying but I try to stop. "*White Jacket* is more accessible," I say.

57

Here's a resting place for me—an all-night laundromat. It has a padlocked washroom, a line of shrimp-colored scoop chairs bolted to a wall.

My doctor did not prescribe enough drugs for me. If that ever was, in fact, his intention.

A tumble dryer is spinning my bandanna and the raggedy shop towels I carry in my trunk

A berserk ringing noise issues from a game machine all the while.

Now a length of red hose untwists itself on the floor between me and the washers, snakes over and squirts water on my sandals and toes.

My car keys are where? They're my only keys. I know I had

them. I *got* here, didn't I? Mightn't those be they, clangoring around in the clothes dryer?

Men Who Are Too Young

"Clean as you go," Hollis tells me. He says this is something he's lived and learned.

He *says* so during this phone call he's made to me at four A.M. Clean-As-You-Go is his reason for calling.

59

After I broke up with somebody and there were no more men, I called an old friend of mine, Lillian, and asked if she might fix me up.

"Oh certainly," she said to me. "Plenty of people."

"Great, great," I said. "So, who're you thinking?"

"Give me just a second."

"O.K."

"There's somebody," she said.

"Thank you," I told her and told her I was hanging up.

"Wait," she said. "Let me try a few things."

So Lillian called around and she came up with Hollis. Grief-stricken and fresh out of his many-year marriage to Midge.

60

Now he and I are watching as some charitable organization pleads away on the television. The spokesperson says that without our donations many Third World children will go blind.

"Where the fuck is my government?" asks Hollis. "Why should this be left up to me?"

He says, "Suppose I don't *have* any money to contribute?"

I don't want to hurt his feelings or make things worse but I have to say, "That, is not too big a suppose."

61

I should be ashamed, though. This is a man who buys, at a reduced price, milk and bags of bread that have expired.

62

We've moved over into my dining room. Hollis is backed up against the wall, measuring his height and marking over his head with a pencil. "You go next," he says to me. "It's fun to do!"

"Can't just now," I tell him.

He's giving me a cool look and preparing a criticism. He carefully pockets his pencil, eases into the chair opposite, stirs the green tea in his steaming cup. "I don't think—" he begins.

I say, "Well, no you don't, do you? You don't think this! You don't think that! Don't relay any more thoughts to me if you do not have them."

63

I don't open the door very wide for the spiteful hunchbacked landlord. He's snooping around to see if I have a pet.

"No pet here," I tell him, which is true, true, true.

64

I end up at the cat shelter. I step inside and announce that I am here for an animal who needs me.

Which is not true if they think I mean any cat in an iron lung or this ET-lookalike with the plate-sized face; technically a cat, considered so by a stringent application of the rules.

65

I say to myself, "Stop it."
Or so I say. It doesn't work.

Ain't Life a Brook

Paulie says he's crying because he's tired and because his trousers are too long. He says they're the only pants he brought to the hotel and they're too long. He's calling from somewhere in Manhattan. I know this from the 212 showing on my caller ID.

There are two cops keeping Paulie company tonight, I hear them in the background. They are Mikey and Rob. "Where are the other channels?" one of them is asking. And the other says, "No! You mean it isn't even cable?"

Simple Machines

I would remind the ex-husbands, "We're still awaiting your well-wishes and cards of concern, your outpourings and bids of assistance. You, who had something or other to do with my son."

68

Paulie's caretakers from the Sexual Crimes Division escorted him to the medical facility where the doctors are giving him TB tests and what all to learn something about his immune system. The Crap-Head Rodent Criminal, meantime, is in a cage at Rikers. That answers a few of my wants and desires. Not all.

69

Now I'm at a mall having indecision shopping and trying to buy something nice to send along to Paulie. A coat? No, no, he's got plenty of coats. What's that leave, then? I can't think. A what? A what? A shower curtain?

70

And with bitterness sigh before their eyes.
And it shall be when they ask you,
"Wherefore sighest thou?" that you shall answer,
"For the tidings, because it cometh."
And every heart shall melt.

—EZEKIEL 21:6–7

I'm at IHOP in a red booth seat, over a swiped tabletop and a Swedish stack.

In the booth ahead, with her back to me, is a woman, her bushy hair under a moss-green scarf. "Just say you're my brother," she tells her companion. "They'll believe it. If they ask you, say you're my brother." The companion is facing me. He peeks up as he pours salt. Should I wag my head at him, no?

Is that the right thing to do or the wrong?

I'm nobody's judge. Not these days, certainly. On my blouse here, for instance, I missed the buttoning sequence by two.

Straight across from me there's a couple on a study date. The male has a loose-leaf binder opened. He says, "Now we'll go through these notes and pick out similarities and differences. O.K.? Here we go: 'Traditional beliefs, customs, laws. Social strife was commonplace.'" He stops and peers through his wire-rims. His girl's Rollerball is wiggling furiously. "Sheila," he says, "don't write the verbs. You don't have to write 'was,' just write 'commonplace.'"

Ah, but I hope they keep it up. I hope they don't load their knapsacks and leave. I hope this stack of pancakes lasts so I don't have to go home and try horribly to sleep again ever. The sky out there is like your head's dunked down in the iodine water. And there are prickly white stars. The wind has tugged up the pine trees and is rocking and swaying them loose.

71

When I try to call Paulie back, there's no answer, he's gone and I guess the people from the Sexual Crimes Division have relocated him for safekeeping in some other hotel.

72

My thoughts about Paulie are a thing, over there, I'll have to go through and sort sometime. Maybe keep some of it separate.

73

Rain batters the trees until they're slick and dripping. There is certainly, outside, a lot going on.

74

And whatever the thing I was looking for, it's maybe in my hand, mouth, on my fucking head, whatever the thing.

75

"I'm at the store," I say to the ringing phone.

Nevertheless, Belinda's revolting voice issues on my brand-new answering machine. "Our edits have been formally delivered. They're on Lionel Shumacher's desk," says she. "Now all we can do is pray."

I don't care what the fuck she's talking about. And Belinda's afraid of chain letters. She shouldn't be allowed to pray.

Are You Sure You're All Right

Daughter Mev lives in a rental, a white house with red shutters and doors. Inside are sunny rooms, gleaming golden hardwood floors.

"Try this," she says, giving me a spoon of something to taste from her mixing bowl.

"Um, I'm not really very—"

"What, Mother? These eggs are like, from hens who were pets."

I say, "There's Methadone in your refrigerator. Mightn't it have an effect on the neighboring foods?"

"You don't get any of this, changed my mind," says Mev.

77

Now we're seated on the floor together and I have a hand outstretched as Mev silently, painstakingly brushes my nails with a coppery lacquer.

There behind her is the stepladder she painted cornflower blue, and stacked on the ladder's rungs are clay pots in which there're hearty examples of the cephalopod plants that grow so very well down here in the country's dumps.

Mev moved here with a Methadone habit. Over a year ago. After she had spent six months in rehab. Which she disliked.

Now, weekdays and Saturdays she rides the Amtrak over the pine-woodsy border into Louisiana, where Methadone can be legally obtained. For Sundays she's given little plastic take-home vials.

Leave Some for Others

You don't want to bother Miss Mev sometimes, she's a very preoccupied person. Anyway, if she were involved in something, you'd have to tackle and maybe blind her to get her to stop.

79

I say to myself, "Whatever it is you think you're doing right now? Lying on the couch there, doing whatever it is you think?

You're going to have to cut it short, know what I mean?"
"Stop *pestering* me," I say. "I have problems to solve. Be with you soon as I can."

But, But, But

"They're replaying *The English Patient*," says the Deaf Lady.
She says, "Which I have to confess I like."
Hollis has such a look of disdain, she adds, "All right, so I'm a sucker for a love story."
"No," I say, "you most certainly are not. *The English Patient* is the most profoundly important movie ever made."
And when Hollis wants to talk I won't let him. I say, "You're only going to say something incorrect about *The English Patient!*"
After he slumps off, the Deaf Lady and I relax and spread out on the bench a little. There is a white sky overhead and a flock of screaming birds.
I'm positive *The English Patient* is a good movie that I too would enjoy.

81

A paperwad pops around in the grass. It blows over my way and catches between my shoes. I snatch it up, undo the crinkled page.
"What's it say?" asks the Deaf Lady. She props her chin on my shoulder so she too can read.
Printed in faint shaky capitals is "YOU WILL OBEY ME."
"Who in the world...," I say.
"Oh, that's the mailman," says the Deaf Lady.
"How so?" I ask.
"It just is," she says. "Believe me. Pay no attention. It's some

Freudian nightmare he's trapped in, you don't want to know."
She takes the note away from me, wads it back up.

"Another thing that happened," she says. "I went to play my
Walkman and found a tape stuck in there. It was the soundtrack
to *Les Misérables*. Show tunes? I never listen to that junk."

"No, uh-uh, that's not right," I say and lower my eyes to
look straight into hers. "That didn't happen to you. That happened to me. Remember my telling you about it? Remember
that we decided Hollis was playing a trick? Do you even own a
Walkman?"

"Well, I do, yes," she says. "However, of everything I've been
telling you, Olive. I found a strange tape. I had a memory that
isn't my memory. My owning a Walkman is not the astounding
part."

I have to ask her sometime who is Olive.

Chapter Three

Just Wasn't Made Very Well

With a glue gun I have attached "Solid Gold" labels to every sort of item.

I pack some of them into a duffel bag and ride them to New Orleans to show the moron New Boyfriend.

Now I get to watch as he hesitates to touch things that are made of wood, paper, rubber, or glass.

83

I have never to this second told the New Boyfriend my home address. I drive to his place; he must never know the location of mine. There was once a mention of the name of my street but I regret that and pray the Boyfriend was drunk and won't ever remember. Which is asking God for exactly nothing.

84

The Boyfriend has advised me from the wisdom of his experience. He's said, "Beer on hard, you're in the yard."

And he was right about that too, as written here with my Lancôme lip crayon on the floor below the commode is: "KILL ME."

Also, down in the kitchen, the box of Rice Chex was opened by the quicker top *and* bottom method.

85

Now he bams on the bathroom door as I'm brushing on cheek powder and yells, "I wanna be at Deannie's eating jambalaya in one-half hour, get ready!"

I open the door and say, "I am if you are."

He looks me over, gives a nod. He says, "You could wear that probably. I guess that's O.K. But you have to put a shirt over it. Honey, there's gonna be *kids* at this place."

86

To them at Deannie's in Bucktown, he says, "Gimme all male crabs."

I Don't Care How Tired You Are

Now he has his "BLOODY DOLL"–emblazoned lighter out on display on this bar's bar. I snatch the lighter up as our bartender approaches. I give my cigarette *more* fire.

88

Oh sure, in my dreams I eat Fritos.

Last night or toward morning I dreamt I ate a full bag. They'd settled but very few of the chips were broken. They had just the right taste.

The Entertainment Industry

Word from my old director friend Penny. He's moved from Paramount over to Mercury Brothers where he'll be working with me and Belinda.

Penny speaks with a lisp whenever he's stressed. Which he apparently is in his new post. He reports that his phone number there is "shix-sheven-shix, sheven-sheven, sheero-sheero."

90

I got started doing script work with Penny. After I met him at some point earlier and then worked with him doing something and then we got better acquainted and by now he's someone I know.

91

To the last script conference, I took my tape recorder so I could get evidence on Belinda.

Here's her voice on my tape saying, "Money. I've received the producers' memo and their response is very bad. But they're not always a hundred percent right about everything."

That is actually the kindest, most supportive and constructive remark anyone at the studio has ever made to me. Girlfriend Belinda.

92

The recording proves to me, however, that in the hours following the script conference when the thing was left on "record" and I carried it around running in my handbag all afternoon, my personality fractured and I became a multiple.

All Characters Improve Their Lot

I ask myself, "So, what's the difference?"

"Well, there is one," I say, "but I don't feel like explaining it to you right now."

94

Mev is here at the sinks, scrubbing fruit for a fruit salad. She says, "With a brand-new syringe, there's a little pop, same as when you open a jar. It's resistance. The release of about a millimeter of air."

Feed Your Head

I play my phone messages for today—thirteen so far from the New Boyfriend. In one he says, "Honey, I've been dipping into the dictionary you bought me."

I did buy him a dictionary. Not an OED, just one that didn't have "Student" in the title.

He says, "Guess it's about time."

96

I go out to the road and sit in my parked vehicle, where no one can disrupt me and people will let me be.

There are street-cleaning sounds, a dog barking in code, and on that lawn, in powder-blue coveralls, a Dimmler's Nursery man watching me, watching me, his lips moving. The sky above us is dove gray.

I hunch down on the car seat but stay high enough that I can keep an eye on my surroundings.

Now comes a gaggle of made-up high school girls in their wide slapping shoes. One with overplucked eyebrows is reading horoscopes aloud from her magazine. Another is asking, "You know what I wish? My biggest wish?"

More on the dark side, I see a dead snake, and by the curb there's a small pile of unexplained cardboard strips on fire.

97

Paulie was healed when I was there, or anyway, he looked normal, in that he could walk and talk O.K., could see and hear. He did plenty of shaking and puking, though. And even if his hands weren't bandaged he could not have held a glass of water to fucking bring it to his face.

Things to Do

The police found the Gruesome Baby Dick Criminal in Paulie's walk-in closet, foaming, and using his teeth to tear the clothes to shreds.

99

I guess he'd like to avoid going to trial and would like to be at home now, doing what he wants with his time, coming and going as he pleases.

100

I dozed for an hour or so, out here in my auto.

In my dreams, it was winter and time to take a sleigh ride. That suited me fine and I giggled going over the icy hills.

Why Bring It Up

I say to myself, "You're not thinking right, you're not thinking clearly."

I say, "You're thinking, thinking, thinking, but most of it is gobbledygook."

102

Each day I make a lot of purchases but I don't unbag anything. If I took stuff out of the sack I'd have to decide on a place for it, stow it somewhere; there'd be another new thing I'd have to own.

Nor am I carrying in any huge sacks of groceries. I'm tossing anything I can't just eat in the car.

103

I'm at the drive-thru window at Aunt Julie's Sandwich, idling with my hand out, about to receive change and oh good, here's the ticken-chuna-talad hoagie I ordered. I wonder what this will *be*.

Bring the Noise

"You can't be my daughter," my mother says. "Who ever heard of a person hating and avoiding sleep?"

"Well, but Mom, consider. I eat jars and jars of speed."

"Why do you?" she asks me.

I shrug, although she can't see, as we're conversing on the phone. "The same old reason."

"Still? I'd hoped you were over that," she says.

"It's a birth defect," I tell her. "Haven't been able to shake it."

105

Whereas my doctor says, "You ought to try taking your medication at *four* intervals and have the effects for *sixteen* hours."

I'm wondering, "From what source, Dr. Rex? A magic hat? Surely not from this nickel bag you gave me to last until summer."

106

"No more journal," I tell him. "I'm never bringing it to therapy again. All my time, any hour, any day of the week, is wasted. Pointless to record where or how.

"Nor am I keeping any more organizational lists. I'll show you why," I say. "Here, you can read this. Its reminders are, one, 'sweater,' two, 'read newspaper.'

"I can't," I say, crumpling the page, "be this pitiful."

And Then a Kitchen Fire

Hollis appears at the door. He says he left work early. He says, "*Fuck* Driver's Ed.," which is what he teaches over at the Roger Taney School, right across the road.

"Lemme in before they see me," he says, and says, "Found out Midge got remarried," as he shoulders past me on his way to the couch.

He lies gaping at the living room ceiling as if an answer is up there, or a picture of a better world.

I sit on this end of the couch near where he has his feet. They're in boating moccasins, the leather laces tied in precise and identical bows.

"Maybe you should go back," I say. "You know how work can distract you sometimes? Just get lost in the routine."

"Always enjoy talking to you," Hollis says. "Always appreciate the many do's and don't's."

"I was in the middle of something," I tell him.

Which I was. I have gone halfway around my apartment with a glue gun, making adjustments, and I still have the other half waiting. What doesn't need glue?

"Have you thought of gardening?" I ask him.

His head raises and he balances it on the sofa arm. Looking at me.

"If you ever start one, you should do your watering first thing in the morning. Afternoon, your plants can overhydrate and burn in the sun. Night, you'll get that powdery mildew.

And you should once a week drown them instead of a little bit of water every day. It encourages deep root growth."

"You are shocking," says Hollis. "I'm not even going to ask if there's ginseng tea left. I already know you drank it, *all*."

"Happy to make fresh," I say.

He says, "A few winks of sleep are what I need. Maybe go grab a nap in your spare room."

I've been acting peculiar lately. The spare room has a lot of information about that.

I say, "You can't, friend. Not in there. That room is 'Bikers Only.'"

"I just wanna rest my eyes," Hollis says and lurches off the couch and into the spare room and closes the door.

I hear a crash from in there that is the library lamp falling off the desk. Now there's a pause as Hollis must be feeling around in the dark, getting the lamp righted. In two seconds he'll switch it on.

"Jee-*ruse*-a-lem!" he shouts.

I yell, "Next time heed the warning!"

He reemerges with his head lowered. We bang knees as he steps around me on his way back to the couch. He lunges into place and again lies staring at the ceiling.

I feel an obligation to tell Hollis something. Nothing that begins with "You poor fool." I say, "Give it time to settle."

"Cookbook," he mutters.

"As you wish," say I.

I say, "Or do this. Consider the things you *disliked* about Midge. Her greed and rudeness and disregard. How she treated everyone like servants. That obnoxious and superior laugh of hers."

"It wasn't, if you knew her," says Hollis. "That was all a veil for her lack of confidence, she told me."

"Lack of confidence? How she'd talk about herself?

Nonstop and lovingly? Until her eyes were flaring and her cheeks flushed? She'd claw anyone who interrupted?"

"I'll be fine," Hollis says, sitting up.

"She locked you in that hallway? She pitched a rock at your windshield? She called you a maggot in front of everyone you know?"

"Midge did? Not that I heard," he says and covers his eyes. "Midge said I was a maggot?"

"I could," I say, "*easily* have gotten that wrong."

I'm looking hard at the coffee table, at the butterscotch balls in the candy dish there. Oh, from now on I will keep very quiet.

108

Hollis shakes out his shirt sleeves, buttons this cuff, now the other. "I do feel better," he says.

He finishes with his sleeves and rises from the couch.

"We'll need doughnuts," he says, moving purposefully toward the door.

Capital Not, Capital Happening

And not to whine but the New Boyfriend calls every two or three hours and whatever his crisis, it's bleeding from the nose, it's right away, it costs ten hundred dollars, there's no one else he can contact, I'll have to go to Mexico to be of any help.

110

"Are you listening?" the Deaf Lady asks the whole store of them.

The Few Things I Care About

I sit the New Boyfriend down and explain to him, "I want you to ask yourself each time before you speak. Would your conversation, if you were in the joint, say, be good conversation? Would it be funny or interesting to your fellow inmates in the joint? If your answer to any of these questions is yes, then whatever the thing is, no matter what, you are forbidden to tell it to me."

112

He presents me with a gift from his time in the military—a grease stick of face camouflage. The stick is two colors from nature: light green and loam.

I try streaking the grease on like war paint once, to see how it looks. Like war paint, whatever that really is.

113

"Honey, tell me," he asks now, "why do you think people see aliens?"

My face is in my hands and I'm shaking it. I say, "I'm sorry but go over there and hide from me."

He says, "You don't believe in the people that were taken up?"

"Unable to talk right now," I say.

"No, you're right. That's fair," he says. "'Cause it is my fault for havin' my silly ideas."

I'm silent.

He says, "You don't even believe in such a thing as outer space?"

"No more questions," I tell him.

This Was Your Idea

On the ignition system of the Boyfriend's Jaguar is such a thing as an Intox Interlock. In order to start the car he has to pass a breathalyzer test, which he never can.

So I'm driving but after I make a tiny error he says, "Whoa! Whoa! Whoa-whoa-whoa!"

"Honey, please," he says. "You *must* watch goin' through here. You really have to. 'Cause they're drunk, see, sweetie? Or they just step right out in front like that. They're trusting you. That you'll see 'em and stop."

"I mostly will," I say.

"Bikes, though, are especially bad," he says. "And don't ever, *ever* block the way of the streetcar this way. Fuckin' *go!* That music blasting is what's nerve-rattling. Now slow way-way down, babe, I mean it. I said that they're liable to step right out."

I look over at him approvingly for using the word "liable" and nearly mow down a pair of jogging girls.

"Aw, geezy," he says, "don't go Clairborne Avenue! I already almost got killed there a buncha times."

Dix is his name—Taylor "Dix" Didier.

Back to the crib with him. He has a fifty-room mansion on South Sioux.

I say, "Not too spicy, that dinner you're preparing, Dix. I will be down in your pool."

115

After dark, we roll over to the Saints & Angels Tavern.
The place has a black marble L-bar and on the wall is a green neon trolley full of coral neon people who are waving hello. There's also a pink alligator above a Bud Lite logo and framed glass signs for Amber Bock, Shiner, and Chimay.
"Shiner Bock is brewed in Texas," says Dix. He says this because it is a thing he knows.

116

The man with the woman at the table to our left has forty years of tattoo artistry behind him. He couldn't begin to say how many tattoos he's done, maybe twenty-five or thirty thousand.
He biffs me on the shoulder on his way to the can, and, confusing me with someone, asks, "How's Vardamin? How're the kids?"
"So let's hear it," Dix says dejectedly, once the tattoo-maker has shuffled off.

117

Not one time but three has Dix been jailed for public intox. Chosen from the drove on the streets of New Orleans.
With the same brain he uses to remember to buy milk!
But I have only myself to blame if I listened last night for six straight hours as he argued jujitsu over tae kwon do.
And only me to blame if I didn't speak up before he purchased pink girl things for me for my visits—bathroom curtains, sick with cakey-lace, and terrible little ballerina soaps. My God, what a heartbreaking person!

You Were Saying

I'm here on the bench. The Deaf Lady joins me. We sit silent for a bit, watching what all's going on. There are shadows moving, past the intersection on a lot, of some night staff out on a smoke break. There are rills of steam from a lighted doorway. It's a night after a storm; hot, with no stars.

She says, "Week or so ago, I let the bathwater run over."

"Everybody has," I say.

Now what comes by is a high school bus filled with marching-band members and their instrument cases.

"By a lot," the Deaf Lady says. "So that it drenched the hallway. Ruined the woodwork all along there. Soaked the carpet through. Probably got the floorboards beneath."

"Hmm. Might cost you your security deposit, actually."

"Don't keep emphasizing that," she says. "What do I care about a security deposit? I'm rich!"

"You are? Seriously? How rich?"

"That was hyperbole," she says. "Of course I'm not rich. But the issue isn't some damage I did to the bathroom tore files."

"Guess it's not," I say.

She says, "What you don't understand is, they're putting me in a home. My kids, I mean. Haven't I explained this to you? It's a *nice* home, but that's where I'm going."

I say, "Much later tonight, I plan to take some wine and a blanket, and go someplace and watch the sunrise."

"Take me with you," says the Deaf Lady.

But this always happens. Damn it. Now I'm not sure I want to go.

Don't Bring Yourself Down

Here they are, they're at my door, live IRS agents. Two of them, hammering and pounding.

They say, "Miss! It is to your advantage to speak with us!"

"Well, you couldn't mean me," I say. "I've merely stopped in and I'm just here to see somebody."

"Go away," I say.

I say, "Get the fuck outta here."

I say, "Shoo."

120

They leave me with a card that reads:

IMPORTANT NOTICE. You were OUT when we called. It is IMPORTANT that you visit or phone the address or number shown below. This card is not for ID purposes.

—the IRS

121

Huh.

122

Belinda and Penny make a new regulation. It's that I'm not authorized to think up script changes on my own.

"Write only what the team of us has already approved," says Belinda. "Don't try to get creative. We're not *The Antioch Review*."

123

Seven A.M. and here's Hollis asleep in my living room; his legs under a corner of the oriental and the rest of him covered by a drapery panel he unhooked.

124

He joins me in the kitchen, where I'm trying to scrub this stove burner I scorched. He says, "When you're through with that, you think we could have Cream of Wheat?"

He sits down and watches me from the breakfast nook. He yawns.

I say, "I've been scouring this now for an hour. It costs what, three hundred dollars?"

"Never mind that," he says. "Listen, you woke me up with your humming. That Dial soap jingle? Do you keep that kind of thing in your mind? What if Malcolm X heard you humming that?"

I say, "You're *back*."

That's All Right, the Girl Will Get It

An article on missing pets advises me to drop pieces of my clothing on street corners all over town. The article asserts that my cat will be drawn to the scent, have a seat, and wait for me.

I take the suggestion and I'm willing to sacrifice for my cat. A lot of my wardrobe goes out of my life this way.

126

I tell myself, "O.K., I promise I'll shut up but there's just one additional thing."

"For*get* it," I say, "no more commentary. I don't care what you think."

127

I run into my friend Martin over at Red Lobster and say, "'Quarter to Three' by Gary U.S. Bonds. Now, there was a dance song."

I say, "'If I Was Your Woman' by Gladys Knight and the Pips."

"It's not rated," he says.

I say, "Well, don't you think it should be?"

"Don't you think it should be?" he says, doing a cruel but eerily accurate imitation of my voice.

128

I drive down to New Orleans and here's Dix with his arms wrapped in black electrical tape for me, and his clothes have immense and several zippers.

So I'm deciding I should go somewhere else—nowhere, but definitely else.

Chapter Four

129

For the world's so dark without you,
and the moon's turned down so low,
and I get so lonesome about you,
way in the night, you know.

—James Whitcomb Riley

Posted on the rear of this truck is the sign: "STAY BACK 50 FEET." This cautions me that the truck might fling its cargo of glass shards and sharpened metal spears.

Everyone on this road is a twat. This road is a twat. A word that should be retained for its utility.

I take the Battier exit, get off the interstate, swerve onto the access road, pitch my sunglasses out onto the pavement, line the car up, drive back and forth over them and back and forth thirty-nine times until they are ground to powder.

130

I know now that nothing I planned is going to happen. Whatever it was I planned. Gum! I meant to buy gum. Why was that so impossible?

This Must Be America

Battier's convenience stop has no food, no coffee, no cigarettes, no sodas, no gum, and nobody who wants to wait on me anyway. So this is turning out to be a great day.

Outside the store, a man in a white apron and a white paper hat sells me mineral water, newspapers, magazines, a fresh tomato.

132

"People liked Neal Cassady," Hollis says to me over the phone.

133

Talking to him can be a hell, friend or no.

I say, "Just answer me straight on this one thing. Would you want such-and-such?"

"That's a whole different situation," he says. "I can't address that."

"But would you? Honestly?"

He says, "It's completely different."

"I know! I'm asking you to make a simple comparison."

"No can do," he says. "The two don't compare."

134

I say to myself, "Take Tylenol. I don't want to put up with your asshole whininess."

"That's nice talk," I say. "Very compassionate. Impressive vocabulary too, I might add."

"Asshole whininess," I say.

135

Rifling this copy of *Rolling Stone,* I say, "Here's a full-page ad for the U.S. fucking Army. And do I hate Jann Wenner for running this ad? No. It's they who don't write him letters saying, 'Cancel our subscriptions, Butterball. You better rethink!'"

136

To this truck I remark, "Archway, you're psychotic. I don't know if you've had too many cookies or what, but choose a lane and drive in it."

137

I rumble over the Alabama border into Florida. I have thought not at all about where I'm going. I wouldn't turn back, though.

138

I would give Paulie this fresh tomato, pat his curly hair.

139

My headlights glance on signs with silhouettes of moose. "Look for moose," I say to myself. I say, "At least back there you didn't hit an armadillo. And you had the option."

140

I drive under morning stars along the Perdido River, through thirty miles of barrens. Now and then a barn's side advertises maize or syrup or something else I wouldn't buy. I should turn back. Florida is a horrible toilet. There are a zillion snakes woven into this road and those clouds over there mean God's coming.

141

That fat man driving around with his little pooch? Now why don't I know him or someone like him? That man, I bet, could make me very happy.

142

Can I turn here? O.K., good. I can? Thank you. But what if I don't know if I want to? Sir?

143

I just regret everything and using my turn signal is too much trouble. Fuck you. Why should you get to know where I'm going, I don't.

144

I would say to some ex or other, "I never liked you. I know you were back in the back there, with all my favorite photographs, blacking out the faces, scissoring off the heads."

145

I'm taking a room in the next town, whatever is the next town, and moving into the room to live there until I die and be among new and different people.

146

My room is in the Villa Rimy, a place dressed with scarlet shutters and nestled along the sea road.

I sit at the window, elbows on knees and not moving but looking out, thinking this evening I'll jog on Boulevard Je to the old port and the city wall and run past that to the parapet and see the blackened fort. I'll go at dusk when the streetlamps have smeary bowls of light and the sky's bubbling and everything's brown, dusted over, baked like pastry, when the wind's still searing but there's no shrieking sun to contort things and make them see-through.

What I have is no real interest in running but a little bit of wonder that my mind can house such a mélange.

Chapter Five

Pay the Man

We're in a tavern on the Riverwalk, Boyfriend Dix and I. He slows up to lean over a table of people he knows. "She's forty or so," he tells them too loudly. He says, "But she is, up and down, a wonderful-beautiful woman."

"You're set for another six months then, Dix," says one of the friends at the table. "What're you supposed to do after that?"

Over here in the corner, two of the waiters are sipping from a helium balloon before calling out their food orders.

Stay Where You Are, Don't Come Any Closer

"You're saying?" Dix asks me.

"What I'm saying," I tell him.

"But you mean?" he asks.

"Same as the words mean," I say.

150

Now he's regaling me with tales of his days in the United States Navy. He says, "You berth a ship, sweetie. You park a big ship where you deep-channeled—you know how they throw those big huge ropes? Those are four and a quarter inches in diameter."

151

He teaches me how to flip my Zippo lighter from hand to hand. He's an idiot but he knows the one good trick and now I know it.

A'ight

Mev and I are seated across the table from each other in the breakfast nook. We've been coloring Easter eggs. Mev's too miffed at me to speak. She snatches up an egg on which she earlier crayoned "Mother" and prints above that, in angry caps, "I AM STILL YOUR."

Stuff My Mouth with Gas-Soaked Rags

There, I've created order. The next time I want aspirin it'll be in the bathroom closet on the second shelf in the sixth row beside the other pain relievers. Right beside.

Also, I've now painted everything in the place, everything, especially the hideous mint-green spine of this Thomas Pynchon book, which I do someday intend to read at least some of.

I've painted the stapler. That and my little travel alarm. The cleaning supplies and vitamin bottles are now Venetian gold. Jade green and lavender blue *complement* Venetian gold. So does a very deep yellow.

One problem, however, is I'm no longer sure if I have a lot of something or a little. Before shopping, it'll be necessary to hand-weigh every item on the shelves.

And on the keyboard, I shouldn't have coated gold on the numeric keys. The alphabet I can touch-type but the ampersand is where in the hell?

Letter to Sean Penn

I get off a letter to tell Mr. Penn that I rented his movie *The Indian Runner,* and that, although a few scenes seemed stupid, the movie was otherwise enjoyable and well worth the time and trouble it took to watch.

155

I say to myself, "Wash the hands first. Dinner started at six, you're late, sit up straight at the table, no you may not be excused."

I say, "Do you think you could pour that without *spilling?*"

For hours and hours.

I follow myself outside, asking, "Where do you think you're going? Are you finished with your work?"

I have to admit, "No."

"Then you're not allowed out, get back inside," I say. "And hang up your jacket."

So I guess I'm not going anywhere. But what's there to do at home? I pulled the plug on the television.

No Fun for Anybody

Hollis looks up from his magazine, reaches and flicks something off my shirt collar. "Onions on your blouse," he says.

Why can't he make it easy for me? *Why* must he make it so hard?

Still Don't Know What You're Talking About

I let my mother into my head for a minute and she's—what do you know?—in there giving a lecture on pharmaceutical marijuana.

I say, "Damn it, Mom, I said they should do that, back a long time ago. You yelled at me!"

158

Now it's the CD player. "I'm goin' down," sings Mary J. Blige, over and over and over.

Vocabulary

I'm crabbing at Dix about the blinks on my answering machine
that have appeared since I went out and came back in. I say,
"Twelve messages in eleven minutes, Dix? That constitutes
stalking!"

He doesn't know "constitutes," so we get off on that and we
never return to the harassment issue. He likes the word for its
government sound.

160

In this one message, he's wishing me a "Happy Good Friday."

The Streets Are for People

I'm at the head of the line at the water company bitching my
head off and making a very good point and I would be *winning*
this argument if I had it *with* the water company and not with
the electric company which is where I ought to be, way down
on the opposite side of the avenue.

I'm Sure Someone Can Use It

Mev and I colored a psychotic number of eggs and made Easter
baskets for Hollis and the Deaf Lady.

Now those two couldn't be happier. They're curled up on
my couch chuckling and nibbling candy at one A.M. as I traipse
off to bed.

I notice that Hollis separated the yellow marshmallow chicks from his basket and put them into the missing cat's sacred bowl. He's saying, "Milk chocolate rabbits are delicious."

Mustn't Keep Them Waiting

Now, is that noise me? I'm slowing down, letting everybody get away from me until I determine if I am the cause of that noise. Or if my tire's on fire, that fucking thing, it's my least favorite tire. And this bridge is not correct. It took me twenty-six minutes to find the wrong bridge? I need to be in Petal in one-half hour. Or no I don't, I'm not going to Petal! Or I could go to Petal if it's anywhere *near* here. On the radio is the loneliest piano music.

I'm vibrating. I wonder why I'm not driving somewhere to eat? I could have stayed home and ignored food totally.

Enough of this! I need Jimi, Van, Black Uhuru.

Below is oily black water and hurrying over that are long night tugs that are webbed with tiny purple lights.

164

I can close my eyes and, if I ever want to, go back in time and hear Paulie rehearsing for the dipshit school play, singing in his little sixth grade voice that he had then.

165

I say to myself, "Damn you, damn you, God help you, help you, help."

Men of Science

"Just getting a little background on you," says the doctor in Admissions at the nut hospital when I try to check in. "Where did you attend high school?"

"Oh," I say, "just skip ahead, will you? Ask me something from now."

"All right, whatever you prefer. Marital status?"

"That doesn't matter either. You can leave that blank too."

"Last menstrual period?"

"Look," I say. "Life has its problems. Those are not they."

"Well," he says, "I don't want to seem impertinent."

I say, "I am guessing that no one does."

He has his clipboard slotted between his knees now, and he gives a sigh. He holds his pen aloft, like a dart he's going to throw at me.

I say, "Just ask what you need to ask so we can both get on with it. I'm busy, I'm sure you're very busy."

"O.K.," he says, "let's start with what brought you here. Tell me about that."

I nod. With this I'll comply. I say, "I have an awful, kind of, Sunday hollow feeling."

"Yep," says a voice to my left, the voice of some other applicant for admission here. I like being understood but I wish this hadn't happened.

The doctor isn't going to let me in, anyway.

He doesn't care that, on the way over, the skyful of silvery little fish almost made me wreck. Or that all the other cars kept getting ahead of me, even though some of those drivers never gave a thought to Sylvia Plath.

I want to explain a few things before I finish here.

"This," I say, pointing at the area in front of me, "is not my real life. My real life is still coming up. It's just a matter of my digging in. I won't have this hair, for one. I'll put better magazines out. Drink juice. Take stuff to Goodwill. Get the car tuned. That, there, will be my real life."

It's Not What You Asked For

I would say to one particular ex: "Twit was too short a word and Pigboy was unkind. I should never have said such ugly things about you. Bumpkin, however, and Thieving, Lying Wino can stay *right* where they are."

Filing System

O.K., scary. Out this upstairs window, whatever just flew by on its wings was fur-covered and bigger than a fox.

I say to myself, "Think about something else, you'll be fine. Put on a nice robe. Movies! Find something with Morgan Freeman!"

169

The phone rings as I'm stretched out on the bed now trying like hell to remember where I could've hidden the Morgan Freeman films. The answering machine catches some female calling here for Hollis. "Hollis," her voice says. "It's me...."

I know that one. Through and through. And I know everything "It's me" is about.

170

The thing rings again, I grab it up. Mev is the caller. Mev, who is off visiting Nimrod or whatever is my dad's name—her grandfather.

She says softly into the phone, "He's been pointing questions at me, Mother. Interrogating me for information about you. But just hold up before you lambaste me. I didn't *rat.*"

"I am still his daughter. Maybe he's just curious."

"Nuh-uh, none of that," she says. "He can forget about it. Your whereabouts at the precise date in time? Get a warrant, Grandpop."

"I've always liked you," I say to her.

I'm Just Here to Fix the Furnace

"Here's the answer," Hollis says. "No, listen to this, listen. Just yank out those idiotic shoulder pads and the coat'll be great."

"Doesn't have shoulder pads," I say, flopping dejectedly onto the bed.

"Well, then *done,* it's already great," he says and throws up his hands as if his words were supported by logic.

172

I wander into the kitchen to make peace with him after a while.

He's standing at the stove stirring some mysterious potion he's got bubbling in my little copper-bottomed saucepan.

I ask what he's doing and he says, "It's obvious."

I tell him it really is not and he says, "In a few seconds we'll have pistachio pudding."

So I think I've changed my mind and I can never make peace with this person.

Get the Bugs off Me

"Where was I?" I ask myself, just out of bed in the morning.

I say, "Three clues. Not at Pizza Hut, not in outer space, not in New Jersey."

"That still doesn't tell me, though," I say.

174

The hardware store's on strike so I have to beat it over there before the workers form their picket line.

From inside the store I see Hollis trailing after me. Or that he wants to. He means to. But, no. He gets stopped and brought into a discussion with the strikers and now there he is, grabbing up a protest sign.

175

I wander the store, pick up a trowel, a level, a toolbelt. This pegboard in front of me, it's hung with what? Rafters, anchors, nutcrackers? I don't know.

"Show you something?" asks a salesman.

"I just need wire," I say, "I guess."

"Any particular kind of wire? That does *hedges*," he says. He takes a tool away from me and realigns it on a shelf.

"No, just regular wire. Whichever one people buy the most. Your most popular."

The salesman stares down at his feet, lifts and turns each of his shoes, this one, now the other.

176

In the yard, the Deaf Lady.

I call out, "You should see what they have over there," and, arriving before the bench, jostle my bag. "Like a staple gun. My dad always had these, but he'd make me leave the room before he used them, and my husbands were the same way! They'd say, 'Those can be tricky, honeypie. Better bring the thing to me.'"

"I'm never sure," the Deaf Lady says, "when you're faking."

177

Two white boys approach from the side yard. They're sporting fresh haircuts and wearing shined black shoes, blue trousers, starched shirts.

We watch them walk over to my apartment door. They thump the knocker and wait. Hollis answers and lets them inside.

What Did You Think Would Happen

He's in my living room, down on the floor petting a little collie dog I've never seen before. He's performing for the Christian boys, who're trapped on the couch now, observing him with the dog.

He says, "There, there, Molly. Everything'll be fine. I'll get you to the veterinary hospital the moment we're through here."

"Sir, we can *go*," says one of the boys.

"I'm sure there's plenty of time," says Hollis. "Let's get back to that thing you were telling me about Paul and the Thessalonians."

"That is not his dog," I say.

"I feel sorry for it, though," says the second boy.

Hollis raises himself slightly and looks at me. He says, "Darling? Maybe think about changing your blouse before we leave?"

I come back out of the hallway, where I'd begun shelving my hardware things in the little utility closet. "Why?" I ask him. "What's wrong with my blouse?"

"Now, now. Don't get huffy. You have plenty of nicer things you could wear," he says. And, softening his voice, murmurs to the Christians, "With all the money she spends on clothes?"

"It's funny but *I* bought a blouse like that," says the first boy. "And gave it to my mom for Christmas."

Gives Me the Shivers

Daughter Mev lights out, bored at her grandfather's. She calls me from Snowshoe, Pennsylvania, at four in the morning. I'm up. She calls from a phone booth near the boiler room where she's taken shelter. "I didn't plan this greatly," she admits. "Like I've got all my meds, safely ensconced, but I should've stopped someplace and stolen gloves or mittens."

180

Five in the A.M., the phone jangles again. My heart goes roaring up my throat.

"We were disconnected," says the Boyfriend.

And I'm hanging on the line here for a minute or two. This ploy is so good, I'm letting him talk.

"I'd just like to come visit my lady love," he says, trying to wheedle the address out of me.

He says, "I don't see what's the problem. Is it our age difference?"

"Enough about that, you can drop that," I say. "I've been lying all along. I'm the same age as you."

"I thought you were much-much older," Dix says.

I wait for him to apologize but he's not going to. He's an idiot! He says, "Honey, this is a huge relief. Here I thought you were like really-really old."

181

Last thing before sleep, *I* get to make a call. I dial the phone and recite some favorite movie lines as a message on Hollis's answering machine. I say, "'Dad, I love you. But you think of yourself as a black man. I think of myself as a man.'"

The Issue Is Not the Issue

Church of the Sacred Passion, I get right up next to it and to its pastor, who's out here glad-handing.

"What was your name again, dearie? I'm sorry, I know you've told me," he says.

That is jive. He's never asked, I've never offered.

"Linda Kenesevich, isn't it?" he says.

I go inside the church and get down on my knees and pray. "God, please, you must hear me. Please don't let me resemble

Linda Kenesevich, the Bougainvillea Blossom Cleaners' manager. Please, God. I deserve better respect than that, for who I was in the day."

Hate to Keep Asking

"Up! Lordy! Good morning, I'm up!" I say. "What the *hell* has been going on?"

Chapter Six

184

About the Mercury Brothers' script I think: O.K., get a lot of sleep tonight, war starts tomorrow. You're going off to war. A plane will take you to the war place and a limo will fetch you so you don't gotta worry about parking. And when you get through, even the first day, you'll be able to leave war and relax. Maybe go out, have cocktails with somebody, chill and put war out of your mind.

Nevertheless

I notice that at night before landing at LAX the plane takes a little side trip and we're over water dumping our fuel. So dangerous is their imbecilic runway.

186

Like an electric football game is their runway. All the parked planes jitterbugging and lurching cattywompus.

187

"That," explains our pilot, Captain Butterfield—and what a handsome all-business kind of fellow he is—"was an earthquake."

188

I have purchased a soft pretzel and I am eating that as I await my ground transportation.

I say to myself, "How smart is this?"

189

My director friend Penny is an exacting man who knows food temperatures and tire sizes. For getting to the hotel, he gave me nineteen minutes' worth of directions.

But my driver, when I try to give him the details, says, "It's four streets."

Along the way the pretzel topples me. I'm streaming and saying, "Let me out of here!" but to myself mostly and I mean my own skin.

The driver fits something onto the seat beside my face. "Here's a bucket if you feel like you're gonna get sick," he says.

And I'm out of it, but that bucket was once a tub for Imperial Margarine.

Work Better, Go Union

I ask myself, "What time is it? Seven or so?"

"Actually, it's a little worse than that," I say, peering at my watch. "More like seven-fifteen. You're late!"

"All right, I know," I say.

I say, "And whatever you did last night? It must've been disgusting. So disgusting you passed out in terror."

The Something Producer, Evan, ended up here, I'm fairly sure. And the night *did* cost me but somehow it paid very well. Here is my wallet, emptied of every dollar and coin. My left Nine West shoe, however, has six hundred bucks in the toe.

191

I say to myself, "And let me remind you. The next time you go off in some *purple fucking haze,* you are not to go wearing your good red-leather jacket. Because you don't always return to consciousness with it on. You know what I mean?"

Whether I Matter or Not Doesn't Win or Lose

I'm at Mercury Brothers, given not even a chair but a stack of boxes to sit upon while Belinda chides me.

She says, "Perhaps you won't mind if I tell you what I think. I'm talking about the *work* we expected from you today."

"Right, right, I know," I say.

"I'm sure you know," says Belinda. She swats open the script she has on her lap and swivels in her chair so she's facing away from me.

"That everything?" I ask.

She looks around at me for less time than it would take to

check a clock. She says, "When I went by your bungalow last night, I noticed an auto parked outside. Perhaps you're not a person who treats her schedule very seriously."

"So, is that it?" I ask.

"And if I'm not mistaken, he's married."

"Who?"

"Evan."

"Producer Evan? Could be," I say. "Plenty of people are. *Are* we through here, Belinda?"

"We're going into a meeting," she says, and now she's yanking pages from the script. "Into a meeting. With *this*."

Hell, as far as I'm concerned, has frozen over, and I'll soon enough be living in an underpass in a cardboard box. "Get you," I say to Belinda. "Get this woman," I say into the air.

193

The script used to have a man in love with a wood nymph. Then a version had him in the redwood forest in love with a tree. Now the story's set in Alaska, and is about some dame chasing after Bigfoot. My job, and what I do for a living.

194

There are eleven producers around the meeting room, groomed and golden men wearing cuff links and three-piece suits that cost more than my car. Their assistants, or whoever's assistants, are going in and out to fetch mineral water for people. They're neutralizing us with ballgame/train crash/scalp massage talk that is unrelated to work.

Now, I don't have the nerve to ask if anyone fell by my bungalow last night, so I'll just go on. There are other things to mull over. I see a few. Mr. Shumacher's eyeglasses, for one. Are they not upside down?

195

For an hour, Mr. Shumacher has been reading to the group. Perhaps a thousand pages! He finishes and his brow lifts. He sips from his smoking cup of tea. He turns to Penny. Penny turns to me. We contribute nothing and so look to the next guy, Evan.

Whom I now remember seeing at some time this morning. I needed the washroom. He was in my path. Could that hick have given me money?

All of Evan's remarks are around the theme of his happy marriage—when he and the wife did this or went there or had such and such happen.

196

"Don't start on me," I say to myself. "Yes, I'm deeply, deeply regretful and ashamed."

And No Fat Chicks

Penny tries to keep a lot of control. He would not mix a red rubber band in with his beige ones, say. Or if he suddenly knew that in his wardrobe closet there was a shirt facing the wrong way, he would vault from behind his desk, cry out for his driver, and be sped home.

198

He and I are in the glass-block building that is Studio B, in the sitting room Penny prefers to his office. The room's got two floor lamps, a couch, camel-colored walls. It's a plain, uncomplicated room.

We're seated on either end of the couch. Penny holds the laptop and in there is the script. I'm allowed nothing—not a pencil, not a pen.

Tilted against the wall opposite is Penny's mammoth bulletin board. It's tacked full with index cards that have scene directions, slug lines, notes in Penny's creepy little insect scribble. Although I like the man. Now he rises from his seat, ambles over there, reads something, unpins the cards, switches them all around.

While I'm slouched here, wondering what attracts me to this work. Nothing that is good, that's for certain.

Penny's in close, his shoulders bowed as he tacks the last cards. He's wearing suspenders today and an immaculate suit. "O.K., not bad," he says. "Not too shabby."

I say, "It's excrement. Vapid and cornball. Trite, boring, insipid shit."

Penny's round head gives a nod. He drops back onto the couch. He isn't listening. At least, not to me.

199

I wander down to the cafeteria, get a scary orange-iced bun that's not worth unwrapping, get coffee, droop over it, think about the mistakes I've made.

200

I find a phone, call my daughter Mev's place, leave a message for her on her answering machine. I say, "Did I forget to tell you this? Don't live your life in the gutter!"

Not Deaf

Back in the sitting room, Penny reads a line aloud for me: "'After descending Mount McKinley, Justine trudges through the—'"

He says, "We need a better verb."

"Wades through," I say.

He won't look at me.

"Marches through," I say. "Or, moves."

He says nothing. His fingers are stopped, frozen in the air over his keyboard.

I say, "She lugs herself. Drags herself. Kicks through. Pounds. Tramps. Traverses. Treks? She journeys. Advances through. Treads. Marches. No, hikes. She pushes her way. Shoves. Rambles. Roams. Wanders through. Backpacks? Ranges? Strides! Paces! Stomps! Walks! On her *fucking feet!* Through the *fucking snow!*"

202

There isn't a right word. I can sit here doing this until my periods cease. And I can keep in mind that Penny's the easiest person in show business. Especially compared to Belinda, who's coming up next.

203

"What was that name you told me this morning?" I ask her.

"Yesterday. You mean yesterday," Belinda says. "And it was *Renquist*. I'll get you a goddamn pencil."

"No, no. No need for that," Penny says.

There's a pause as we wait to see who'll win this tiny point.

"I'll remember," I say, although that is not likely. It would do to keep things bopping along.

204

What I'd like is a brandy, heated and served in a snifter. I'd like it brought to my table in the corner booth at Joey's in Fair, Alabama.

205

These scenes are set in the Chugach Mountains and in the Independent Mine State Park, where there are gold mines still, and people panning for gold.

"Could you look up the *term* for what they're doing?" Belinda asks me. "Before you scratch 'panning' into the script?"

"Ah, I beg your pardon?" Penny says. "Belinda? Our character is a nurse practitioner? What interest might she have in gold?"

"Audiences like it," Belinda says.

"I don't," I say, because I don't want to look up panning, and because I hate Belinda, and I must just *want* to get the sack.

"That ish show totally out of character," Penny says.

Ask to Speak to Whoever's in Charge

I telephone Hollis, who promised to look after my place.

He answers the phone with two words: "Dryer's broken."

He says, "Not to worry. I took everything out and hung it on the line."

"How can that be?" I say. "I don't have a clothesline."

"No shit," he says. "You don't even have a rope. It's all right, it's fine. I just unplugged some things and strung their extension cords together. That did great, for all the fucking trouble it was."

I say, "I might be heading home soon. I'm right next to getting the boot."

There's a pause from his end. When Hollis speaks his voice is low and muffled. He says, "I hoped you'd give me a little *warning.*"

I don't ask why. With all that could happen between here and there, I may never need to know.

207

A leaf-green cab streaks out of the traffic and, just beyond the studio gates, slows up for me. I'm running.

208

Each and every tire squeal reminds me I lost my cat.

209

I don't ever tell Paulie, "I'll take care of you." He's heard that one. He heard it from me, my parents, his sister, from each ex, from his friends, his doctors, his church, his school, his employers, the neighborhood, the police, the mayor, the state and the federal governments. It wasn't true.

Everybody, Step to the Right

This bungalow has a gargantuan television and *Peter Pan* is the movie on Home Box Office. I'm watching along when the film's narrator announces that the Tinkerbell character's fading. To prevent that, the guy says, I should clap my hands.

I watch all the way through to the end, without clapping. Tink's resurrection is just *one* of the lies that movie's full of.

211

Now, about this child telling the eleven o'clock news, why did they shear its hair off and make it wear brown lipstick?

212

The bungalow has a phone system and the Boyfriend calls me on it. I answer and pretend I don't know him at all.

"Certainly *sounds* like you," he says.

"Well, I am like me," I say.

213

I feel around in my handbag, extract something, use it, and put it back. Later on I might need something else. *This* is my life, what my life is really made of.

214

Radio on or off, I hear it.

215

I say to myself, "Almost four hours ago, you got that pill caught in your throat. You'll want to catch another one in your throat in five minutes."

216

Now I don't remember anything. Nothing. Well, I remember bits of this and that but not much.

And sleep was when?

217

There's an anemic moon out there, milked over, hanging low in the low green sky.

That couple in the heated pool. How do they, I wonder, figure into things?

In here there is Danish Modern furniture, lampshades that look Western. It's all like it's for a hunting lodge, not a nice one. Rubbery drapes that've halfway derailed from their crappy rods.

218

It isn't anything but as I'm writing my notes for tomorrow I fill up a page and don't turn to a new page. I just press down hard with my pen and write over top of what I've already written.

I'm going to kick that fucking TV into the road.

219

I can fit the palm of my hand between Paulie's eyes. I know what it feels like to do that.

That man hanged him. For one thing. Had him hanging. By the neck.

Chapter Seven

Where Are You Taking Me

We're into the third hour of this meeting. Belinda's speaking, gobble, gobble. Maybe I haven't heard every word.

I'm dead tired, dead stupid, I can barely talk, so if she calls on me I'll just fill in with something authoritative and use like a radio announcer's voice. She does call on me. I say, "Sixty-two degrees and there's *traffic*." Laughter from the folks around the room. Not from Belinda. The others, though, shifting positions and some taking seats on the carpeting now, as if they were watching a little fireworks display.

She hands me an outline of her many, many changes. She says, "We'll need the revision done tonight."

I say, "To*night?*" and she shushes me.

I say, "You mean *tonight?*" and she grabs the thing back.

222

She has me moved out of the ugly bungalow and over to the Hollywood Patio Hotel, which is a lot worse as it's nowhere and it's certainly not in Hollywood.

She sends messengers to the door every couple hours. They're all heavy drinkers of, I would guess, wine. Named Elton and Cyril and some other name. They're to spy on me and make sure I'm working, to repeat Belinda's commands and make sure I'm alone.

223

The hotel is near nothing, and when I've complained about that almost enough, Belinda has the messengers deliver tubs of food.

But this food is from EST or it's for Reverend Moon's followers—great huge buckets of chips, pretzels, inch-thick sugar cookies.

Immediately, the diet has me rethinking things and reevaluating some of my attitudes. For instance, all people are nice, if you give them half a chance. And I should be more disposed to obey the will of others.

Kick That to the Curb

Belinda catches me as I enter the vast lobby at Mercury Brothers. The floor here is black marble. The glass lampshades, pink. She's seated on a plump suede settee. Around her is the latest class of note-taking interns and assistants she's ridden and driven blunt.

She keeps me standing and gazes at me, her one eyebrow raised, the other frowning.

She rises, saying to her group, "I must set something up with Deiter. Hold your places, everybody." And, as she brushes past me, says, "I've had a *very* angry call from Ian Anderloche. Which you and I will need to discuss."

I'm sure the interns heard this. They're miserable now. They don't know where to look. I'm standing over them, anticipating that one might want to ask me about something. But no, it's unlikely that any of them will.

Somewhere near, a loose window frame keeps dropping and every bang makes the interns clutch and startle like they've been shot.

I bum one of their pens and a slip of paper so I can leave a note of explanation for Belinda.

"Dear Faithless Back-Stabbing Ingrate Mongrel Whore," my message would read, if I had legibly written it.

225

O.K., there's Valium. That is one fine drug.

226

The studio has assigned me a car and a driver who's nicknamed Tick. That's nothing he need fill me in on at all.

Tick has a second, lower-down job shampooing pets. Yet I don't get the sense that his combined employment pays adequately, else why isn't his car a color I can make out? Or heated? And why's it got straw sticking up where the back seat was gouged and vandalized?

But none of that is my business or anything to cry about. Not like the repulsive fact that "We Won't Give Up the Ship" is on autoreplay in my mind.

Shoes Dyed to Match the Bag

Ian Anderloche, the executive producer, is asking, "What were you up to here, Miss Breton? Can you tell me? Because no one ordered this scene change that they remember." He's raised out of his chair and leaning over his desk, holding the script open to me like it's a wad of flowers I wilted.

He'll get nothing from me.

He wags his head, falls back into his seat, puts a thumbnail between his teeth, sits looking at me and waiting.

"Lemme explain something," he says at last. He swats the script around to where he can see it. He reads, turns a page, reads.

He's maybe twenty-four. Wearing his hair buzzed. Wearing the khaki clothes of a photojournalist. He has his sleeves rolled on his arms, and there's a pack of Kools in the breast pocket of his shirt. Not opened properly, that pack of smokes, though, as he ripped the whole top away.

"Unless someone orders a scene change there shouldn't be a scene change," he says. "Some one of my people. We don't proceed that way unless one of *them, orders* a change. Don't go by your opinion. Is that what you were doing? You weren't hired for your opinion. We decide all that. We tell you when a scene is wrong. So don't take it upon yourself. Don't ever do that, if that's what you did. If you, personally, didn't think something was funny."

"Wasn't funny," I say.

"We have three, different, media experts. Who've done viewer research and demographic studies. Have all their findings. They tell us precisely what's funny, what's sad, what hits home."

"Neither did it hit home," I say.

But I may've hurt the feelings of Ian Anderloche. He's shoveling the script into an envelope. He's enunciating. "Certain things, have been, established. Certain cultural truths, exist. Like it or not. Agree. Or not. We have learned. In our business."

When learned? I wonder. He was playing with his Darth Vader doll when this old script came about.

228

"So...," Penny says. We're over in B-Building, in the reception area outside Belinda's office. I'm sure I look pale and exactly like a beggar.

Penny nods at the envelope Anderloche gave me and says, "In there, the script you used to be working on."

Ride Along With You

"Monica," Belinda says, beside me in her limo. My real name's Monica. Big fucking deal.

"What project will you go to? If you're released from Bigfoot?"

But she's already smearing the question out of the air. She says, "I'm silly to think you *have* a plan."

I agree that Belinda is silly.

I say, "So, does that mean..."

"I don't have that information. Stop asking me," she says.

"You really, truly don't?"

"What have I just told you?"

"Belinda, I need to know."

"What were my *words?*" asks she.

"All right," I say.

We ride. I turn my face to the window. I'm ashamed of myself for so very many things. I say, "Maybe Penny will have heard something."

"You'll have to take that up with him."

"Although you were the one in touch with Anderloche."

"I just *detest* you," she says. "To the point that it's almost invigorating."

We slow and the driver steers onto a lot for a produce market. I've told him I want to be let out here. I need to supplement Belinda's tubs of pointless food.

It's half dark even though there's a yellow sun through the leaves of the queen palms.

The limo steers off. Inside it, Belinda turns in her seat and gazes out at me.

Now Is Not the Time

I'm dumped into an orange armchair, back in my room at the Hollywood Patio. A couple of actors glide into view on the TV screen. They look like Paulie, or how Paulie used to look. The one in wide-wale corduroys especially. Curly hair. Pretty teeth. Dimples. "God d*amn* you," I tell the television before I smack it off.

What the hell kind of drug do I take to get out of this moment? I would go up, down, or sideways.

231

One thing to do in this grotesque hotel room is prop up on the bed pillows in the middle of the night and yam down a hundred stick doughnuts.

Keep in Mind

Penny's voice message this A.M. is: "Itsh a mishtake to provoke theesh people. Shtill, the fact ish you have a point-shistum shtep contract. Beyond any one produsher's authority, and, wishish, beshides that, not in Ian shintresh to dishpute...."

233

I get busy and decorate the script with Alaskan details. I put in Caribou people, the Aurora, Toutketna, the Iditarod. I have Justine wearing tattoos and a Mohawk. Going dog-mushing. Wearing gloves to disguise her black, frostbitten hands. I put Bigfoot in long johns and a short wool parka with a flannel hood. Show everybody smoking stubby cheroots.

Because this stuff *adds* to the script, I'm thinking. From now on, that's all I'll do. I won't cut anything, I'll just add.

234

"O.K., this isn't working," I say, slapping the thing shut. "Maybe reapproach this at another time."

"Won't work then either," I say, switching off the desk lamp and climbing out of the chair.

I wander to the window, look out at the day.

"Never hurts to try," I say.

I say, "Maybe not for some people. For me, yes, it does."

"Learn to *cope*, Pattycake," I say through a sigh.

Plenty of Time for That Later

The girlfriend of some ex told me, "You'll find someone else. I know you'll be able to. A person with all your energy?"

That is what she left *in* about me.

I thanked her!

She said I was welcome!

She asked, "What lies did he tell you about me?"

"All there are," I replied.

Promise You Won't Laugh

Now a meeting with Anderloche, Shumacher, Belinda, me, and a few others—Evan and two, I guess, assistant somethings, Janice and Jonas, and Crumley, who's Belinda's whatever-he-is—I can never remember and I'm barely here and the introduction process isn't all that organized.

"Let us attempt to define and hopefully answer the studio's first concerns," says Mr. Shumacher. "Shall we?"

Belinda leans forward in her seat. "Specifically," she says, "they need to know, what is lovable about Bigfoot? If anyone can suggest. And next, how do we get that across?"

"Maybe he's half Lancelot. The other half *brute*," Crumley says.

Janice says. "I don't know if this makes sense, but does anyone else picture him as an innocent? Like a boy who never grew up?"

"I think even if he strays, he really loves Justine," says Evan. "Even if his foot slips occasionally."

"How is Marlon Brando a man?" Jonas asks.

Some of us look around at him. *I* do.

This could take days. Several, harrowing days. They need a phrase here. So they can think kindly of the script while I'm somewhere writing it, while they're hiding in their offices not doing whatever their jobs are. "Oh, come on, he's lovable," I say. "He just doesn't have any—" I'm squinting as if the rest of my sentence is far out in space and I'm straining to bring it in. "No Romantic Procedure."

Whoa, do they like that.

They're nodding around at one another.

Mr. Shumacher leans across the table and tweaks my nose. Ian Anderloche pats his palms on his thighs once. He and Belinda rise from their seats and hug.

But just when I'm thinking we're a family, here's Evan, walking off and giving me a cruddy look. I say, "Oh, don't worry, mister, you don't have to protect yourself. I'm about five hundred miles from fucking anyone."

There's More

Once I went to see my mom and Penny was there, visiting. His father and my mother were married at the time. For the very shortest time—a month—before they acknowledged their error. Nonetheless, for that little while, I was the great director's stepsis.

And I was a good stepsister too, as Penny had brought along some dogshit Paramount script he was trying to rehab and I, really out of nowhere, did a bang-up job of doctoring that script.

Of course, there did follow forty or fifty scripts on which I didn't always do a bang-up job.

238

Most of the studios have hired me at some point. Some moved me along. Some let me go. TriStar and Fox each let me go a couple times. But they were fair enough and had their reasons. Like they had to *sit* on me to get me to work.

239

Now I'm lying across the ugly maroon bedspread. Everyone's gone. Flown to Toronto or weddings or another place they didn't say,

I'm just here in the El Patio, haven't yet called the rental people to come collect all the equipment.

I'm admiring this letter I forged from the IRS. It reads: "You are paid in full."

Chapter Eight

The American South

Driving safely away from New Orleans International, if I were in an iron dump truck, would be a neat trick. These people are maybe not trying to kill me, but clearly they'd be indifferent toward doing so.

241

I roar up to a place called Bayou Susan's and purchase Nam vet/Jello shot/gun owner/debutante/Mardi Gras stickers to fwap across the rear bumper of my car. Now, let's see if I'm not treated like an equal.

Protect Your Head and Go Limp

Sixteen hours from LAX to here. I'm trying to finish up, trying to draggle my luggage in off the front porch, especially this Wardrobe Wheeler that just *will* not go up the step. Delta? What the fucking hell did you do to my bags?

Who prowls up and sits there in his car smiling at me but Dix.

"YOUR MONEY BACK!" he calls out.

I slump to a seat on the stoop. I quit, and cannot go any further.

"There's my HARD-EARNED MONEY!" says he.

I probably knew all along this day would come.

"She's MADE OF MONEY!"

Both days. Both would come. The day he'd find me. The day he'd fool around with my name.

And I don't remember what month this is, but whichever, it is too hot.

243

Dix is out of his car now and has his trunk popped open. I just shouldn't look. He's unloading stuff, searching for something. He recommended that I hold still and wait and that's what I am doing. I'm not sure how Dix gets me to do anything, ever. I really have to stop and wonder about that someday and figure out how such a thing came about.

He's thrown onto the ground a Tostados bag and golf shoes and an air filter and a few tools. And, aha! A pair of foam bats is what he brought for me. "Honey, these are Nerf bats," he says. "So nobody gets hurt. We can go ahead and fight with these as much as you want."

Who leaked to him my home address? Was it Bell-Fuckwad-South?

He's holding his electric-blue bats, I'm lying down on the concrete porch, letting my eyes roll back into my head. I wish one of the ex-husbands would come along. This could look like a scene from a Cuban film.

244

Dix says, "You don't gotta worry. I'm not one of those guys gets his rocks off beatin' on a woman."

"God love you," I say.

"You *do* gotta worry, though, that at times I can be verbally abusive."

"No, you really can't," I say. "To do that you'd have to know the language better, Dix. You'd have to know, first of all, what is a verb."

"Everything that you own," he says, "is the BEST STUFF MONEY CAN BUY!"

245

I was already tired and then Dix made me more tired and I shelved my *Tetsuo the Ironman* video in the fridge. The tape seems fine, though, and for the next little while it'll function fine and Dix will like it or be frightened by it and, either way, maybe shut the hell up.

Flower in the Crannied Wall

"You don't *wanna* pay attention," says Hollis and, fed up, throws his magazine at the coffee table.

"Listen to you!" I say. "How could anybody ever possibly argue with you?"

"Oh, *I'm* the one who's unreasonable? Is that it? I'm the one jumping down the other's throat?"

"In fact," I say.

"Yeah, blame it on me."

"Hollis, that is so childish I'm going to pretend I didn't hear."

"Well, we both know you did," says he.

"What?" I say.

"You can't pretend."

"Can so," I say. "Beg your pardon?"

Living out the Trip

Mev is very lovely but I'm not sure about the bicycle she painted egg-yolk yellow or about that—whatever it is—feathered *headdress* she got in Whozitville when she was visiting my dad.

"Fucking hip-hop covers of every fucking song, they're ruining *everything*," she says. "I juss-juss cawled to say how mudge ahh care."

248

"Good job," I say to myself. "Books, music, films, and now the food alphabetized."

249

I take a drive and, using a foot-long flashlight, hunt for my cat, my cat.

*Some*thing white took off running and went behind this house, this wealthy nice house that is, nonetheless, letting off an ugly sound—the dinging, burning, beeping pathological noise of a TV game show.

Just Keep Going Straight

I'm in my car, those two are in theirs.

The woman in the passenger seat is twiddling her sunglasses by the stem.

She probably can't hear me so I go ahead and scream, "You could get your own car! With its own beverage holder! Its own map pocket! *You* would work the controls for the side mirrors!"

251

"You know why you're having this strong a reaction to things," I say. "It's because of those marshmallow pies you ate. Four of them? I can't believe you did that!"

"I can," I say. "No surprise here."

252

See, these people know me. I've been lost in their driveway before.

253

A cop makes me pick up every last cigarette end that I threw onto the lawn of Bell South. Maybe seven hundred or eight hundred butts I saved up. "Hands and knees, Missy."

254

My search for the cat continues. Until after dawn, I'm shining this light and calling and screeching.

And I see now why people like being out in the daytime. The stores are open.

255

I'm going along on Chapel, the one main street in Melanie, my town. The trees are in freakish flower and behind a pink picket fence is a huge fluffy herd of *goats*. The sky rolling over is lavender. At a railroad crossing, a giddy-looking train with a bulbous licorice engine seesaws by.

Whatever You Do, Don't Let Go

Time for a car wash.

Monday morning, and even here at the Econo-Cleaner I have friends.

Party

"What's with the bandage?" I ask the Deaf Lady. "Did you hurt your hand?"

"This? Just a mattress fire."

"Oh, don't tell me," I say.

She says, "Calm down, I made sure it was out."

"When did this happen?"

"Uh, yesterday."

"You couldn't mean yesterday. Yesterday—"

"All right, all right. Then the other day it was," she says. "Get off my ass."

I hear her and deep down I realize that God put the Deaf Lady next door to me for a reason.

258

One thing I have never owned and would never own is a teensy spindly-strapped lady's wristwatch. Why*ever?* When I need to know the *time.*

259

I've spent all afternoon on the photograph gallery here in my office. That shot of me throwing up with Jerzy Kosinski is fine art. I also put a lot into the picture of me with my arm over the shoulder of Joan Didion, signed: "Best time I ever had with a girl." There's a letter I made up from Joan as well, tucked into the back there, in which she talks about drug drops and all the money she owes me.

260

I would say to my ex-husbands, "You know what I get to do? Anything! *Sing*, if I so choose. 'Stormy weath-errr...'"

261

While the thing was under way, Paulie's friend Armando happened to call and he kept calling and trying to get Paulie to answer, only the Savage Lice-Face Criminal wouldn't permit that, but the third or fourth time, Paulie kicked the phone receiver loose and for a few seconds Armando could hear, although he doesn't remember what, but he got the super and got the police and then he must've taken off running and must've run all the way there from work because he appeared at the door, I'm told, panting and breathless and armed with one of his shoes.

Just Go

When I check in with my shrink, he's bleary—as if he's a stand-in for my shrink, someone who's only skimmed my file.

"I'll let you get comfortable," he says to me.

I think, Now that you've said that, I *can't*.

I leave the chair, leave the room, go outside and pace in a circle, have my thoughts, tell them to no one, climb into my car, and drive off in comfort.

263

Cruising the neighborhood. Now ringing the shrink on the mobile phone to make an apology.

"Well, you'd better come back in," says he.

"Oh? And why had I?"

"So that I may be of help to you," he says. "What've you got scheduled for later?"

"Scheduled," I say. "You silly."

"Got *going on* later. At—how about two this afternoon."

"You don't have someone else to therapize at two?"

"I'm begging you," says Dr. Rex. And that always gets me.

264

I take the corner booth at IHOP, where perhaps I can last until two. Thinking about my lean and suntanned son. Weeping into a napkin. Ignoring a short stack and a side of links that, anyway, would be tastier if I ate their depiction on the menu.

I have long thought pharmaceutical drugs were the solution and I was right about that and that's correct. Still, you have to consider, with even the best prescription drugs, who it is who's taking them.

Letter to Sean Penn

In a second note, I write:

Would you have any big objection to my going by the name of "Mrs. Sean Penn"? I've tried introducing myself with it a few times already and it always gets a good reaction.

Yours,
Mrs. Sean Penn

266

Wake up, you drunkards and weep!

—JOEL 1:5

Now we're side by side on the bench in the yard, the Deaf Lady and I. From somewhere we can hear plinking piano music. It fades out. I throw my arm over her shoulder. I say, "Do you want to hear a strange story? This took place in Cumberland, in the fall, back when I was a teenager. It's a true tale," I say, smiling and turning to give her a wink. But the Deaf Lady has gone, for all intents and purposes, deaf.

267

"Get him, get him, get him!" shouts Hollis from the living room. I tumble out of bed and drag in there. He's made a campground on the floor in front of the television.

"Do you *never* sleep?" I ask and throw groggily in with his pillows and blankets.

"They're constantly getting better," says a sportscaster. "Despite the sidelining of their point guard and the banishment of three players from a series of practices. Plus this new coaching team had to learn all-new offensive and defensive sets."

I'm here listening, trying to. That is a whole, other, language.

268

Hollis is six feet or so and he still has the blond hair, and in his undershirt tonight, he's surprisingly fit and strong and Thor-looking.

His things, though, generally, are not very nice. I don't know if maybe Midge took all his money. I would help him buy less crappy things if there were ever a way. His belt and shoes there are definitely cardboard.

269

Once more I'm out, at one A.M., in some store trying to purchase bedding plants. The cashier woman says, "They're three for five dollars. You sure you need eight?"

I'm distracted, looking at this man behind me.

She asks, "You're sure you want to cut it off at eight?"

This guy behind me in the checkout lane is wearing a sweater vest and his arms bare. He's waiting with a hundred-dollar bill to pay for Twizzlers and a porterhouse steak.

Which leads me to look down at my own self.

"Do I know you?" he asks softly.

"No," I say, sighing. "Not in the way you mean."

Dropped Something, I Have to Go Back for It

The phone machine bleeps on and that's my father's grainy voice leaving a message for Mev. She and I are frozen still, not answering.

Mev has on her wire-rim glasses today. Her *head* is still, her gaze fixed on her lap, on some piece of fabric she's embroidering with purple birds.

He says, "Mev, it's your grandfather. Please get back to me immediately. I have something we need to discuss before I take further action. I came upon a most disturbing item hidden in the closet there in the guest room where you stayed."

Mev snatches up the phone and says, "*Listen* to me, Grandpa. I paid forty-seven dollars for that bong. It's personal property.

You weren't supposed to go rooting around in there anyway. Close the door and don't touch a finger to it."

I'm shocked at the way Mev's ordering my dad around. I'm shocked further that she gave him my number to call.

And Me

I remember after the third and final husband left, I looked around to see what was different or changed—two lamps were broken, two chairs, my camera, one of the speakers, a couple windows, a couple mirrors, drawers, cabinets, all handles and knobs, the bathroom, my car, the kitchen.

272

I would like to ask all the husbands, just in case I ever have to fill out a form, "You did *what* kind of work?"

Paulie

I hadn't budged from my chair that first day, not the whole time Paulie slept. I really wanted to talk to him but he was leery of talking. He would rather have swan-dived from the window into the street, was how much he didn't want to talk.

So I sat there with him and time crawled fucking by.

I wasn't even perfectly sure what had happened. All things horrible, I was perfectly sure. And sure I'd never get past it, get beyond it, and let it go. I knew I never would, ever. This was my diamond baby boy.

274

He came to, or he had come to, and it was a while before I noticed. Still leaning over in his chair with his face on the dining table and looking at me, I thought, kindly. He wasn't awake, he just wasn't asleep either.

275

Now I'm choking down Aleve.

276

A news thing with the president comes on the television. He tells the press, "Let's not take the super-flew-us route," and moves his hand in a snaking motion. I think that's wrong in several ways. And I think perhaps a syllable maximum should be set for some people and, I'm sorry, but rather a low one.

There Have to Be Rules

I'm in a bright aisle at Appletree reading a fashion magazine— reading all of it, the letters, contributors' notes, the products listings. I'm thinking, This is not like reading Alfred Lord Tennyson but neither is it like inhaling from a bag of glue.

It's a little like doing glue maybe, as I'm now in the aisle with the kitten greeting cards and saying, "Don't," as a warning to my own reaching hand.

Here even worse off than I is my daughter, wearing the headdress and, as we stroll by the prepared meats, singing, "Eeemo whoa-whoa oh shun."

Somewhere in the store is a little child yelling, "Where's my breakfast?" over and over and over. Mev and I keep turning our heads to the sound. "Kid, it's dark out," Mev says. "You, have got stuff to memorize."

"Mom, no" she says, "bacon kills," as I pick up and put down a package of it.

278

Now she's puking her head off. Methadone's the foulest thing I've ever heard of. She is very, very embarrassed, my Mev, and we're still thirty feet from the car. There isn't one bush along here if she loses it again and, as I suspect she's going to, I've got my jacket ready to hold up as a drape, give her a little privacy.

By That Time, It'll Be Too Late

An article on ADD advises me to put labels on everything in the kitchen.

So here they are, labels. They read: SINK, COUNTER, CABINETS, CLOCK, DOOR, REFRIGERATOR, and inside the closet I've put one on the BROOM. I should be all set. And yet I'm back and forth, back and forth, and Hollis is eyeing me as I seek a stowing place for this net bag of potatoes. Where? Not in the dishwasher. How about if these go sit nicely in the side yard.

"My God," Hollis says. "You need a *wife*."

Chapter Nine

I need coffee bad, and I need a clothes dryer that's free. Over there, Mev, squeezing her fingers into her jeans pocket to find quarters for a giant boy. Now wandering back to the Formica table where she's helping someone fold.

She has sparkle, my daughter—long lashes, soft shoulders, baby skin, the face of a mermaid.

I Was Addicted to Broccoli One Summer

Maybe I shouldn't permit myself even the one cigarette a week. The end went where? We're driving up Corina Street. Mev is shouting, "Hot! Flying! Ashes, in the air!"

She used to have an old BMW that she drove to law school and then drove to the women's penitentiary where she taught street law and learned everything she knows about narcotics. That car disappeared.

I ask her, "Mev? Whatever happened to that BMW you had?"

"Uhm," she says. "I spent it."

282

Late, I drift on over to visit the Deaf Lady, maybe see how she is and sit and have a nice conversation with her.

"So, what's the situation?" she asks, cracking the door.

I say, "I am your dear, dear friend."

She steps out onto the sidewalk with me. She's barefoot and wearing a robe. Which I've done and it's not that drastic an error.

A Mustang zooms by on the avenue, horn blaring.

"We did nothing. Why are they honking at us?" she asks.

I say, "They think it's a compliment. They're men, we're women."

"Then they'd honk at dough," she says.

She buries her hands in the patch pockets of her robe, walks in a circle and comes back to me. She says, "I'll tell you what I hate. Something I've come to loathe. Boating metaphors."

"Really? Huh. I guess they've never bothered me."

She rises slightly on her bare toes and holds herself there. "That you're on an even keel or you're smooth sailing."

"Look what the tide washed in? Maybe that's for a cat," I say.

"You're not a little at sea," she says. "Nobody's a pirate. This isn't safe harbor. There's no ship coming in."

283

I shouldn't be, at this late hour, but I'm up in my room, walking all around, and I've got my hammer but not a goddamn thing to nail.

And I wasted too much time and spent too much time painting in here and painting everything. Yellow and red? It looks like a Midas Mufflers.

284

I decide to phone Dix up and maybe talk to him.

"Honey, you know what's good about me is I all-ways tell it straight up," he says. "I shoot from the hip."

"You don't mean shoot from the hip," I say.

"I sure as shit do. When have I ever lied?"

I say, "By lied you mean, like if you say you're part Mohican. Or you tell somebody you'll give her everything she needs. Or if you say to a woman, 'Wear a miniskirt,' before she picks you up and then later say you meant nothing by it. Or like the umpteen times you went before a judge and pled innocent to drunk-driving charges even though they had a videotape of you, on your knees, in a circus act, were you, in my opinion, lying? Well, Dix, I guess it depends."

I clear the moisture off my forehead. My, I have a lot of anger.

It's all right, though. Dix doesn't even hear the needle skipping.

Same Old Excuse

I don't unroll the Sunday morning paper but fling it, still bound with a rubber band, into the trash basket. I don't really need to know who won the cup. Anyway, here's Mev, seated nicely in the bentwood rocker, seeking my counsel.

"When you're at Grandpa's...," she says.

"Hmm," I say.

"O.K. Mother? May I get this off my tongue, please? There in the hallway when you're going in, right? There's like a gangly hallway table. And he keeps on it these tons of clippings and his memorabilia. So the first thing, he spies me reading some of it. Big fucko deal. That's an invasion, how he sees it. Fucking red alarm, un-totally-believable. Then! Next! Just a couple days later he's complaining that I don't care and don't take any interest in him. Until we're in this shrieking fight and I'm resorted to tears."

She rocks methodically in the rocker.

I sigh. My cheek on the ball of my shoulder. I'm staring at the trash basket and wishing I hadn't chucked the newspaper. I could be reading it and perhaps finding answers in there.

"We all have fathers," I say.

"Yours has a temper," says Mev.

"We all have fathers with tempers."

I add, "Some of them, at various other times, are generous and patient and more-or-less forgivable."

Mev's head turns to me. "So you forgive them?"

"No."

"Why not?"

"The reason all people give. That's how I am."

"Appreciate your candor," says she.

I say, "All part of being a mom."

286

And never mind my father, who did call Paulie "that little goddamned fruit."

Paint It Black

Hollis has paused in eating his chef's salad to read from a literary journal he has lying open beside his bowl.

He strolled over here on his lunch hour just to sup with me.

"Listen to this tommyrot. This individual contends— whoops," he says, snapping a fleck of tomato off his page. "Didn't mean to be messy. Person contends that everything *in* the book, *is* the book. The copyright notice. The dedication and acknowledgments....

"You should read this," he says and throws the review over his shoulder. "Total bull and horseshit."

"I will if you go and get it," I say. "Doesn't sound like it's worth my rising up and walking over there."

Still a Way to Go

Hollis invited me along for this Driver's Ed. session with one of his students—a relaxed-seeming Asian boy named Rudy who wears bulky black shoes and a rope-knit sweater, and who stuck on horn-rimmed glasses to do the drive.

We haven't been touring for long, but Hollis ticks a fingernail on the windshield and directs Rudy to steer us through the intersection and take us for doughnuts at Krispy Kreme.

I do want doughnuts. Or cinnamon rolls.

Rudy goes in with five bucks from me and another five from Hollis.

"You really can't complain," I say, while we're sitting here waiting.

I can see Rudy inside the shop and on the other side of the counter is a purple-faced manager, snarling commands, and a cashier with a gray French braid and a face that is hopeless-looking.

"I mean, Hollis, as far as jobs go?"

"Shouldn't throw stones," he says.

"Beg pardon?"

"I said, 'Shouldn't throw stones.'"

"Yeah, I heard you," I say, "I just don't get the rest of it."

"That is the rest of it, cousin. It means, any people who've been paid for working on movies with talking squash should hide their fucking heads in shame and not throw stones."

289

"Who does this?" I ask, smearing a lipsticked obscenity off the bathroom mirror.

Women Who Can't Listen

Now I've been here at the sinks for a bit, running the tap and waiting for the water to get cold. "It isn't going to," I say. "Accept that."

Another minute goes by and I say, "All right, enough of this. What's wrong with you? Stop. Go do something or take things to the cleaners."

"Well, I would," I say, "but I'm busy doing *this* right now. Doing this, in which I'm greatly involved."

On and on and On

The song in my head switches to "The Battle Hymn of the Republic." I mention this to the Deaf Lady.

"Sing it," she says.

"I can't," I say. "I don't know the words."

"Oh, you do so," she says and sings, "'Mine eyes have seen the glory, dunt dah-dunt duh-dunt, duh Lord. Dunt dah-dunt duh-dunt, the many, where dah-dunt duh-dunt, the sword.'"

So I think I might try telling my shrink the next time I'm stuck with a song but then, That! Is! It!

Life in the Car

Too much speed makes you wince and feel terrible. It's late, I'm lost, low on gas; I'm looking for somebody to blame. I've gotta say this drooling Tropicana truck looks worthy. "Get away from me!" I yell at the truck. "No? Stay, then! We'll both stay. Going faster's the answer? I can do that too." And just let the guy find out for his-own-self that his horrible juice cans are spilling all over the road.

293

Huh. Being driven somewhere, and in the passenger seat of that Ford Covington Victoria is a fully made-up clown.

294

Why am I paused here and in a nervous sweat over these "8-HOUR PARKING" signs? I don't need to stop here for two seconds.

This Must Be America

Dusk, and I'm watching from the window at Dix's place. The night out there is pink and black around a streetcar driver snatching a smoke. He pokes his hands into his pockets, rocks on his shoes. Now his knees bend and he lowers himself to roost on the street curb but no, he bobs back up—remembering, perhaps, his employment.

Don't Want To Know

Paulie had a pill case equipped with a beeper that reminded him to take his meds.

Armando, his friend, said to me, "You know why they returnned him to the hose petal the second time. Headache, from the antiviral drugs. So he was banging hees head."

297

The cops with Paulie change shift every ninety minutes now.

He says he feels like he knows some of them, others he doesn't. He says the weird, disconcerting thing is they're always right there. They'll put a chair over near the door and one of them will sit or more like alight, Paulie tells me, or another one will lean against the wall for almost the whole shift, maybe break away and pace, but go back to leaning. They are all, he says, beat; just beat, every one of them.

He says when they talk it's as if he's a Martian.

He says they're young, most of them, they look like teaching assistants.

He says they're not watching, they're standing watch.

298

"Honey," Dix says now. "You know that thing that was all over the news? That 'Flap over the Flag,' they were calling it?"

I have looked up and am looking at him with both eyes. While from outside comes the clanging mournful bell of an ice cream truck.

"That," he says, "was about the Confederate flag. And about how much it matters to our heritage."

I want to go slowly here. I ask, "What all do you think you have covered under this big word 'heritage'?"

He says, nodding with each word, "It means we did all-ways have the Confederate flag."

I knew he'd say that, or something like that.

Oh, but, man, he is dumb.

I'm staring at the baseboards and at the plug in this electrical socket and at the castors on the feet of this end table.

In another moment I have to decide—talk to him, or leave without another word and speed all the way home.

299

Now, in my kitchen, I'm scouring the stove's burner motherfucking pans.

While floating in to me from the TV I left running out on the sun porch is the low, distant, measured and mechanical sound of an aerobics instructor: "Abs in. The tailbone tucked. Now breathe with the stretch. And, extend the stretch."

300

There's revision work on the script that I have to do.

I've got the last version up on my computer. Juking around and writing Dix into the plot as a demon character.

"He's an enemy of the people!" Bigfoot proclaims, and then I have the two of them face off, eager to fight. "Fool of New Orleans," says Bigfoot, "prepare!"

Broken When I Bought It

I'm sideways on the bed, not feeling so great, and thinking about my many errors.

Where Dix lives they have to start overimbibing and pimping and joining the dirty police force at such a young age. It's not like they have the big illustrated talking encyclopedias in the classrooms, or that anybody very interesting ever drops by to lecture.

302

This morning he's out on the front porch, twisting and turning the doorknob.

He's brought, he shows me in the palm of his hand, little novelty dice that spell out, "I SORRY."

Those I get to keep.

Chapter Ten

Kick out the Jams

I think part of the drag of being lost is that it's called that.

But I am endeavoring to find my way, aren't I? Perhaps I overlooked the exit for Violet or perhaps Violet wasn't the exit to take. I'll just journey on.

304

Now, with this couple here in the gold Ford Taurus I sense strain. Her chin's tipped up and she's looking to see if he's mad and if maybe she should say something, and he's shaking his head, no, there's nothing wrong, although his face is a sour mask of regret.

I pray, "God, hear my plea. May I please never have anything to do with anything like that ever and never participate in that type of thing again."

305

Penny's down here already, fooling around and fishing out of Point Gilbert. Where I've been before with someone. It's swamps. Kept at a hundred and twelve degrees and it has prehistoric birds.

306

He and I are supposed to meet up and do a lot of work and then fly on out and present it to Belinda.

Because wherever we are, we're on the payroll.

Still Think They're Cheating Me

This spooky stuff along here means I'm going the right way—smoking crawfish shacks, rubble yards, a dead tire place or two. There are stalls and stands selling all the bait and voodoo fish hooks you could ever want to own.

However, these people here get the *sun*shine.

308

Weirdly, my hotel room in Cerulean is nice. Vases of flowers. A white piqué coverlet on the bed. Shiny dark wood floors. Lace at the old windows. Ah, but there's always one-more-thing, now isn't there. Left below the bed for me—a baby's Stride Rite shoe.

I'm wondering about it, as I'm in bed and preparing for sleep, telling myself it's fine that a terrific baby stayed here before me and there is no reason to believe the stay ended in tragedy just because the baby left behind its shoe. There. On to the next thing. I'm wondering, when do you ever see the truly attractive Christian men? I want to ride to church in a black van full of French-ski-champ-looking Christians. That, to me, would be the way to go.

I'll Keep Quiet

When I was staying with him, Paulie went out and leaned on the counter in his kitchen and read the ingredients on a dozen different teas he had, with his white-gloved hands picking up and turning each box one after the other. I said, "You've been looking at those for almost an hour," and he said, "Well, right, but I want to know what's *in* them," and he didn't give it up and he tipped yet another box into the light, saying, "So I can find out if this has like...lemon grass."

As though he'd been able to turn the sound down for a time.

310

I'm trying to hold on to the situation with him, but I've got a scrap of something in one hand and a scrap of something else in the other.

The Entertainment Industry

"So, do you fish?" Penny asks me, calling from his room.

"Sure, I do," I say. "What could be to it? You have a pole, sit by the water, the fish come along."

"Actually, it's a little more organized than that," says Penny. "We have a guide."

"Oh," I say.

"Two guides, in fact. They're Cajun, but you can understand most of what they tell you. We're leaving out of Port Hero at five in the A.M. so out of here at four."

"I'll still be up," I say.

He says, "Remember to wear stuff that covers you pretty much head to toe. You don't wanna get eaten, or sunstroke."

"Well, never mind, then," I say.

"Aw...you sure?"

"I am," I say, "so sure."

Momar with His Kids on Fire

Belinda joins us suddenly. And, as I don't like thinking about Belinda, the question of why she has appeared, in my mind, never comes up.

"What a pleashunt shuprize," says Penny.

"Wait," I say to Belinda. "You mean we don't get this time off?"

We definitely do not and I am aware of that. I need to know if Belinda will strike me.

313

Now she's saying some words I'm not hearing but the way she's speaking is like she's ripping a paid bill in half.

Although, I've been perched here at her side being so nice and nodding along, pretending she wasn't repeating everything for the fourth time.

She has my latest rewrite of the Bigfoot script—with the evil demon character—resting on her thigh.

She waves a hand over it like it's a smoking trash fire and says to me, "I don't want to do this now. I want to see some of New Orleans."

"O.K.," I say, "great. Me too."

"Who could take us?" she asks.

"Penny."

"Penny's out in the swamps."

"No one, then. We take ourselves."

Belinda gives me a look that is utterly disgusted.

She asks, "Where's your husband? Didn't you have a husband?"

"Left me for a dumber woman," I say, which is true, true; he did, true.

"Hmm," says Belinda. "Maybe smart or dumb wasn't it."

"A bigot and a Republican. Selfish, whiny, and mean."

"Breasts?" she asks.

I say, "None whatsoever."

I say, "Still, it's a mystery. What a girl like that could see in him."

314

Belinda went to bed early, so I've wandered out and found a nice, normal bar. Oak booths. Sports photographs. Ceiling fans.

There's an eruption from outside the place and a couple of sopping drunk men crash through the front entry and onto the tiled floor. They're socking each other on the shoulders and neck, grasping each other's shirts, throwing themselves off, scrambling back together.

I've been, since their arrival, a cactus.

"Get out of here," someone yells and someone else yells, "Yeah. Go."

I don't mind these fighting men, is the truth. They're not going to bother me tonight. They won't denigrate my efforts, or ridicule anything that's mine, won't roll their eyes, or correct me, or cut me short and leave the room. They won't burden, or overwork me, or heap upon me responsibilities that are theirs. And, no more than they are doing, they won't intrude on my privacy, try to embarrass me or make me uncomfortable.

Plus, they seem pretty far beyond hurting each other.

You Can Fly But Your Body Can't

My first seat was in first class between Penny and Belinda. Before I poured Rémy Martin down my throat and had to come see what the folks in the back here think of things.

316

"Cool out, you know I didn't mean it, I don't really hate you," I hear someone say.

While, over the intercom, the pilot jabbers. He's explaining that some dysfunction, once we're on the ground, can be easily fixed with a pin. I don't know, at that point, how much any of us will care. Maybe I'm drunk, but seems like they could give the plane to the Arabs once we've all made our connecting flights.

317

The beer nuts just served to me in a cello packet are the most delicious food I've ever tasted in my life.

Back at Dallas–Fort Worth I put an Otis Redding CD into my player and I doubt if I'll ever have reason to take it out.

Through the window, trigonometry, under a silky pink sky.

Why Pay More

The Hotel Dioria is a grand stone structure. I got here by way of a slender drive that was bordered on one side by a row of white statues and on the other by a lineup of cottonwood trees. I've just docked my rental car in the valet lane and now here are uniformed employees at my service.

I wish I were wearing and carrying the nicer clothes and luggage of someone better than I. These men are helping with my *duffel*. To know the time, I'm consulting my UNICEF watch.

319

My behemoth suite is ordinarily for—I'm guessing—a child star. The décor is like a day care center: primary, bright, natural, rounded, sturdy, durable, stain-resistant. I could splash cups of espresso all over and mar nothing. I could stamp burning cigarettes out on this floor.

I say to myself, "Ah, but that is not what you're here for."

320

My work is there, with the machinery and equipment the studio's messengers delivered. Software as well, still in boxes and jewel cases and shrink-wrap.

Mercury Brothers spent for this stuff. Belinda would have put me in her cement basement and she would have said, "Are you using that new steno pad? I haven't heard a thank you!" For Belinda is the tightest of wads.

321

"Don't convert backslash characters into yen signs" is just one more thing for me to ponder.

Look Better Than You Do in These Pictures

Penny opens a desk drawer, squints at something in there. He says, "Uh-oh." He could be seeing anything—a stray staple or a Canadian coin.

He is such a fresh-faced, Howdy Doody–looking guy. Always in the madras shirts.

His best movies, however—*Millicent, White Wine,* and *Don't Do That Again*—were three of the finest American films of all time.

So here we sit.

323

He makes me work through lunch, throughout lunch, at the lunch table in this sushi restaurant. And I don't get it with this food. What would it take them, two minutes, to cook the stuff?

324

I have to remember, regardless of anything I've espoused or told my kids, that what matters out here is not how good a job you do; that's unimportant. What matters is how your hair looks and all your expensive clothes.

Cyborgs at the Gala

So I've dressed my best for this studio meeting.

However, woven and stitched into the bodice of that executive woman's sweater are rosebuds, and they're still alive.

326

All of the liars at this conference table are referring to "my second reading" or saying, "on my third pass through the script." Are they psycho? A John Ashbery poem you could read three times, maybe.

327

The only thing I really have going for me is my attention deficit. It's very, very impressive to these people. How I forget to collect my checks, or fail to kiss the ring of whichever the hell one is the studio president.

On the debit side, I missed removing an electric roller this morning and did the sushi lunch and the studio meeting with it lodged in the back of my hair.

328

"I'm sure you regard yourself as a nonconformist," says Belinda.

"No, a good beatnik," I say, with a tap of the tip of my pen.

History Says

I'm trying to read because I have to be ready to discuss these two scripts in another hour with development folks from Universal, or perhaps they're from MGM, I should learn.

I do have their jillions of pink phone messages organized alphabetically in a packet.

This first script involves the twelve apostles after Christ left them. And I see right away, in one glance, that Saint Matthew has undergone a gender change. This babyish fucked-up fucking town.

Script Two, titled *Shitstorms and Peckerheads,* is for what— boys?

I've said it before, I'll say it again: I can no longer be a part of, or go on in, or have anything to do with this business.

330

I have to keep notifying Armando with all the different hotel information so Paulie can find me if he ever wants to find me. And maybe call if he ever gets a chance.

What a Rip

There's something wrong with this day, and with every day that I've spent here. Work, lunch, a cigarette, and they're over. "You're kidding me," I say, each night before sleep. "That was it?"

332

I believe everyone alive should have to watch the news, but it's acceptable to watch the news WITHOUT SOUND. You see planes in flames and bandaged heads and they make as much sense as they're ever going to anyway.

333

The IRS takes all my money,
Bump-bah,
Gotta borrow from my honey...

That is the refrain from one of Bigfoot's original music compositions.

All We Do Is Argue

I say to myself, "Very funny. Very, very funny. Fucking with the clocks..."

335

There, I just ate all my idiot food. Although my meal would've been more enjoyable if the couple behind me had lightened up. They criticized everything—the weight of the silverware, our server's shoes! I don't know how they digested their dinner and I mean there they go, angry.

336

I'm reading through the latest printing of the revised Bigfoot script and I say, "Whoa, wait, wait, no, no, wait. This is all fucking wrong. This has *pages* missing. What happened to the action scenes where he ambushes the demon and throws him into a trench?"

Belinda. That apple doll. Someday I will go where she is and set off a bomb.

337

Now she's summoned me to her office and has me standing like a halfwit in the center of the room.

There are polished hardwood floors, a lineup of lemon trees before the tall windows, cushioned loveseats covered in Laura Ashley prints, a tiny but authentic Frank Stella painting of which I won't someday mind owning an imitation.

"Money, has it ever occurred to you," she says. She takes a sip from her cappuccino and sets the cup back down unhurriedly. "That I know precisely what elements I want in the script? That when I say 'golf' I mean he's to play it. Not something else. If I want a canoe and a romantic moon and a ukulele, I'll have those too. What makes that so impossible for you to understand?"

"Nothing," I say. "Canoe, moon, ukulele."

"Be quiet," she says, and shifts back in her chair.

338

I need to do something very right.

What happened? Used to be, someone would come over to your place, put a cool cloth on your head, offer to pay for it.

339

I'm walking by Penny's office where the door's ajar and I can see him in there, stoop-walking with his hands and arms reaching like he's trying to catch a duck.

340

Out of the Hotel Dioria, into the Forty Winks Motel.

We're at War Softly

I say, "I'd be happy in this room if I had a dust mop."

"No," I say with a sigh, "that is not true. It wouldn't end there."

342

I've been, all afternoon, propped with both bed pillows on this Elvis-ish couch.

I broke down and started eating items from that fucking appliance—the Special Executive's Refrigerator. I'm into their

'Cocktail Snacks and Appetizers' for pretty big money. Although I would like to say in defense of myself that a couple things I ate only out of curiosity.

Paulie

"There are a lot of reasons that people don't take care of themselves," I say to Paulie. "Or that they stop taking the best care."

He's phoned me here at the Forty Winks, upset because a woman cop made remarks about his appearance.

Which is, I take it, deteriorating.

He says, "Although I, you know, worked as a model. And used to get these like two-hour haircuts. But what she's talking about is that I don't even want to bathe."

"Paulie. Hold it. Stop right there."

I'm seated on the side of the bed, bent over as if to tie my shoes, phone in one hand, kneading my forehead with the other. I say, "I don't think anyone but your doctor should speak to you about personal hygiene. Including me. That is a very, very private matter."

"Yeah, but she's just trying to help. And I don't know what's wrong or what're the reasons," he says.

"And yet there are some," I say. "There's how awkward it is with the gloves and all. Or, that maybe you don't *want* to feel attractive."

I say, "And there's thinking of yourself as somebody's toilet."

344

Rain's thrashing against the motel room's picture window. The white dawn and the rain have tinted everything a heather green. On a piece of poster board, I've inked in a huge crude calendar. Now, first thing out of bed, I'm marking an x through today.

Chapter Eleven

Wear a Sun Hat

I've finished hoeing a little rectangle of earth in the side yard. I say to myself, "I'm about wiped out. You?"

"Nah. Not for another hour."

"You're the boss. So what's the time?" I ask.

"It's now twenty-five," I say, tipping the face of my watch into the sun, "twenty-eight after."

"It couldn't be. No way possible. I've been out here much, much longer than that."

"I assure you," I say, reading my watch again, "it *is.*"

346

Appletree hires Mev for the Meat Department, to wrap and package chicken.

I wasn't sure at first and asked, "They are paying you? It's not just that some chicken there needs cutting?"

347

Secretly I fear she'll arrive for work on her yellow bicycle or wearing the feather headdress of which she's so fond. That they'll fire her and think she's nuts. So I drive her to the job every A.M..

348

And as I am still her mother, each day I dispense to her a few pieces of parental advice—"Sleep and you'll feel rested." "Read and you'll be smart." "Lift weights and you will grow stronger."

There seems so much to cover. I hope Mev holds this chicken-cutting job solidly and for a very, very long time.

349

See me in this black-and-white photograph, shoulder to shoulder with Albert Camus, both of us smoking, both with the collars turned up on our identical peacoats.

What Do You Need to Know

The Deaf Lady says, "*I* didn't set it up for the neighbor dogs to bark like that all *night* fucking long."

"Probably they had my cat," I say.

"Oh, what a horrible way to think! More than horrible—macabre."

"Nevertheless, it's what I envisioned."

She says, "You must keep that separate in your mind from what is real."

"Thank you for telling me that," I say, genuinely relieved and grateful.

And What Else

I find Hollis on the floor in my living room, two unopened Power Bars on his lap and a gargantuan reference text lying beside him. I tiptoe in my socks around his study area. He glances up and says, "Wearing your...Thumbelina clothes?"

I say, "These! Are! Pajamas!"

I stretch out on the sofa behind him and look at yesterday's paper, see what I can see. He turns halfway to speak to me. I elbow up and lean forward to hear.

He says, "Neon. Picture it like a straw. Except there's gas down inside there."

I nod, flump back.

He starts again. "That's really all clouds *are,* is gas. Or gaseous water. Humidity. Steams up. Makes clouds."

"So, what's a kiloton?" I ask him, just for something to do. "Or maybe you don't know," I say.

He turns away from me and plucks up a Power Bar, tears at its wrapping.

"Sorry."

"Weight," he says. "It's a thousand tons, equivalent thereto."

I'm going through the newspaper, or so I pretend. "Hollis?" I say.

"What? Hollis what?"

I drop my arms and rest the paper, look over at him. "All this that you know. It doesn't make you better than me."

"Than I," he says.
"Still doesn't."

O.K., But Where Are You

I'm parked outside the grocery waiting for Mev as a threesome of retarded adults approaches the automatic entrance. They come to a halt at a fresh flowers display, jam the electric door and set off the noise of a nasal buzzer.

And down there's a man wearing the store's red singlet, throwing his shoulders into pushing thirty shopping carts.

Now I see Mev, by the Toy Corner, chatting and with her arm over the shoulder of some absolute derelict.

This is her striving to do good in the world, and one more way she worries her mother.

353

At the women's penitentiary, Mev taught, such as, how to open a checking account, or read a rental lease, how to register to vote, subscribe to a magazine.

354

With her earnings she's bought staples and in bulk. "I'm all pre-pared," she says. "In case there's another World War Two."

I always understand Mev. I have to go up and around the corner with her sometimes but I do understand.

What Makes You Think So

"Aw, this is a fuckin' ginger snap," says Hollis and tramps back into my kitchen.

356

Mev visits after work and sits with me on the sun porch. She's wearing cat's-eye dark glasses and sipping from a wax-paper cup of lemonade.

"Don't ever eat chicken again," she tells me.

"Really?"

She nods. "Really, really don't. Very much to your detriment."

"Heroin's one thing," she says.

And What Did You Learn

My cat is back. Quacking and faking blindness but back.

358

She's here before us, lying on an elbow if that's what it's called.

"She's *mammoth*," says Hollis. "With a huge butt. Was she always like that?"

"Truly," I say.

"What's her background?"

I say, "Loped in on a Saturday morn and sat down."

No Fun for Anybody

I say to myself, "Don't put that there, you're going overboard."
"I don't agree," I say and hang the macramé God's-eye right, smack, dab in the front window. Walking off, I call out, "That better not get moved."

360

"There's a trick to this part of the vacuuming," I tell Hollis.
"Which is?" he asks, sighing and seeming low on patience.
"O.K., you don't ever go back there behind the couch. The cat has stuff stored back there."
He's looking at me.
I say, "It's her house too."
"You could train her. You could teach her to pick up her goddamn toys and put them where they belong."
"But I *have*," I say. "She *did*. They *are*. That *is*."

All Characters Improve Their Lot

"Sit down with me," I say to Mev, patting the couch seat next to me.
"I can't now, Mother. I'm so hot and tired. I've gotta get these poor shoes off my feet." She stands with a hand on her hip, the other opened on her thigh. "What's so funny?"
"Nothing." I lean forward, square up the magazines on the coffee table, fall back.
"Mother, you know that pressboard?" she says, nodding at the bookshelf across the room. "Because of whatever it's bonded with, it spits off poisonous fumes."

I say, "I never asked you, Mev. What kind of law you were interested in."

"Torts," she says. "You need to set about two or three plants all around the shelf. They will, for some reason, absorb up the toxins."

362

"Maybe he's quit drinking," I say to Mev, on the subject of an ex-husband. "Or at least maybe he's cut way down."

She says, "I could take only *mini*shots of skank."

363

"It's a noun," says Hollis, consulting his dictionary. "Meaning ...'civil *wrong.*'"

He says, "'Skank,' I've looked. It ain't in here."

364

Mev's fired for having had her eyebrow pierced. I drive over there to fetch her.

Her eyebrow is *bleeding* when she gets into the car. I say, "You need vitamins and to take vitamin K! What kind of a slacker junkie were you? All junkies know to take vitamin K. It helps their blood coagulate!"

"Mom! Mom! I will try to do better," says Mev.

She has, I now notice, a violet star-shaped barrette pinned in her hair.

365

Hollis is perched on one of the seats in the breakfast nook as we come in. He's eating a pecan roll and reading the Book of Revelation. "Whoomp!" he says. "Did you ever *know* about this? 'There will be no more night.'"

366

In my head now, the mixed-up words to rallying war songs. Do you never get to sort through and wipe disk that stuff?

367

I drop onto the bed, grab a magazine from the nightstand, gape at the cover, set the magazine down, reach and unlace my boots and flip them off, scoot back on the bed, plump a pillow behind me, balance the little blue phone on my lap, elbow up and position the phone back on the stand, get up off the bed and pad barefoot down the hallway to the kitchen, slide open a drawer, feel around and find the nutcracker, flap open a cabinet and snatch the bag of pecans, carry it to the bedroom, stand gazing for a second, flick on the overhead fan, sit cross-legged on the floor and pop open the bag of nuts, get back up and fetch the little metal wastebasket, sit down, jump up and clasp the TV remote, punch the power button, get seated.

"Your wife divorced you and remarried while you were still in a coma, isn't that correct? It must be hard to describe the feelings," says the TV.

I scoot around so my back's to it, hold the remote over my

shoulder and work the mute button, close the bag of nuts and twist its end.

368

I say to the cat:
  "And don't think I don't know what you're doing.
  "And don't you try to pull any tricks.
  "You better open your ears, little lady.
  "And don't you give me that insolent look.
  "I've got bigger things to worry about than you and your shenanigans.
  "I better not have to chase after you again.
  "Haven't I tried to teach you obedience? Do you even know the meaning of the word?
  "You stay in that spot until I'm through speaking.
  "I've warned you and warned you and this time you're going to learn."

369

What did you go out to the desert to see?
A frond swayed by the wind?

—LUKE 7:24

From Paulie I learn he's been relocated again.
  He tells me that each of the hotels where they hide witnesses has been spilling over with protected guests.
  He says that every morning, crowding the elevators and bustling out of the lobby, are a hundred persons dressed in court clothes and accompanied by agents and plainclothes cops.

370

The Nightmare Snake Parts Criminal has friends and associates stalking Paulie. Or so it was heard along the grapevine at Rikers Island. Where there are undercover people who find out things and who tell.

371

He would tie Paulie up and hang him some way or other. Take him down and rape him. Hang him up and take him down.

372

Paulie is not supposed to talk about things, or think about things, or try to fill in anything he's forgotten. He's to do no writing. Anything written down is evidence that would have to be shown to the *defense*.

373

Whereas, the results of the Spitwad Criminal's HIV test may *not* be used as evidence in a trial.

This Is What Takes So Long

Paulie looked real for a moment, when I was there at the table wanting to talk to him. But something disturbed him and his gaze switched sharply as if he were catching part of a terrifying weather report.

375

Still, he woke me one night to show me something through his telescope.

I had forgotten how beguiling is Paulie.

And Yet

My sun porch TV says, "I can tell you it's a marionette. Who would walk with strings just like on the show. With a wooden body...."

I Should Get Going

Good, the cop behind me is a child. Those may be his horn-rims, that may be his real nose, but the mustache, fake as could be.

I wonder if the young officer is planning to give me credit for however many of those orange cone things I've clipped because, come on, man, I got most of them.

378

Stores! Stores! So what is there to go in and buy? A yellow something? Another briefcase? Sugar Babies?

Look at these phony people, driving four and a half miles per hour in the school zone. Theirs is the same Chevy I saw in the alleyway, zooming ahead to hit dogs. Jeep, stop tailgating. Do you imagine this speed is convenient for me?

379

Sixty seconds inside Super-K and I'm faint from the fumes of the cleaning fluid with which the alcoholic workers are over-dosing the floors. Also, the two aisles leading to the Electronics Department are roped off and I can't go evaluate any of the electronic crap I shouldn't buy. Twenty-four-hour store, my butt.

380

I haven't done my laundry and I'm down to garbage-picker clothes. These other late-night shoppers however are far, far too well attired for this store.

381

I'm in another all-night place, seeing if it's any better. It is, and I would especially like to own these one-hundred-eighty-one-dollar trousers. These are nice, worsted-wool, great trousers. Pen out, I draw a little "S" through that first digit and make it a dollar sign.

382

Driving home, I'm seeing this dirty fucking sack of trousers on the seat. Now I'm a person who *steals*.

383

I don't go anywhere, I'm merely out here practicing going somewhere, cruising the neighborhood, and I can't imagine what people think. I'm neither a cop nor, at the moment, someone with a pet missing, yet here I am.

384

I stick in this Bob Marley tape and men are making U-turns and others running out of their homes to get to know me. A word to the wise.

And Don't Call Me Doll Baby

With his hands on his hips, Hollis shouts at the cat, "You come back here!"

I'm close by, in the breakfast nook, forcing myself to eat a grapefruit. "That doesn't work the same with cats," I say.

He huffs into the living room, throws himself onto the recliner and shoves back, raising his legs with a clunk. He says, "She knocked the whole g.d. stack of *Progressives* onto the floor, and I just had them sorted. Look at that! And there's two more she already clawed up. Hidden behind the couch or wherever she takes them."

386

Kids erupt from the elementary school building at Roger Taney, across the road, and a few dogs arrive to bark them aboard their navy-blue bus.

387

I don't want to think about Paulie. I don't want to think about Paulie. I don't want to think about Paulie.

Who Are You, Really

"Not there, not there," I tell the cat. "Sit on anything but my final William Morris check."

389

"You think 'Yankee Doodle Dandy' is about what, coming out of the closet? I'm pretty sure I do," Hollis says.

He says, "And can I make a deal with you? Enough with the honeysuckle candle, all right?"

I Know You, I Know Your Heart

"So," I ask myself, "what's next?"

"Ahh, you know perfectly well what. You're to sort the travel receipts and take them to the accountant."

Asks the child inside me, my alter ego, "Couldn't we do something else like a tea party or go race bumper cars?"

"Well, no, we can't," I say. "Because I don't have patience and tolerance for such stuff, for things that are, really, for children. For even an intense game of Chutes and Ladders, I do not have patience. TV is right on the edge."

"Then I guess there's nothing to do but *work*."

"Your guess is correct," I say.

391

I'm swallowing a new medication and Mev, standing before me, asks, "What dose?"

"Don't know," I say.

"Consult the bottle," she says.

"It says thirty milligrams."

"Whoa!" says Mev, rocking back on her shoes. "Are you gonna have the nightmares. I was freaking on seven point five.

"That Neurontin they gave me at the detox place? Oh, man. I couldn't *see*. Plus it made my hair fall out."

"You don't want be blind *and* bald," says Hollis.

"No," says Mev, "but they just line people up at the nurses' station and you have to swallow whatever's in the Dixie cup. They're mostly beige."

"Well, I would be *too*," says Hollis.

Voodoo for Windows

I find a website for the NSA and send them an e-mail:

Dear National Security Agency,
what's it like 2 work there. i think i might be available soon,

if U R interested. Let me know if there's a brochure U could send. Maybe I 2 could B 1 of U.

And then I'm nervous as hell that some NSA bag of shit will think me immature.

393

Another attempt to teach my printer to do envelopes. This is my, what, seventh printer? They never learn. I might as well be asking my coffee pot.

One effect of the new medication is a line of thought that goes, "Trouble always passes...."

394

"You *don't* ever have to do without electricity, for Lord's sake," says Hollis. "If they ever turn it off, you just follow the line, take the cover they put on there, and throw it away. You never touched it, never saw it, you don't know what it looks like. But what you also have to do is, you have to plug in the little two diodes or dinamodes or whatever they're called.

"And then," he says, "just disappear back into your house."

395

"Help me think like Bigfoot," I pray.

I'm staring at the page, at my pen, my moving hand. There's thunder and I say, "I *am* Bigfoot."

Just Don't Be Mad

I was playing with the cat—throwing things and she'd chase after them—and by mistake, whomped her with a walnut.

I've gotten onto my knees to apologize. I say, "I'll buy you anything you want. Or I could take you someplace. Would you like to listen to music?"

397

"Something tells me I need a nap," I say.
"That would be your brain," says Hollis.

But, But, But

Mev, at the door, says, "I heard about the cat. You want me to try and talk to her?"

It's drizzling out there and Mev and her bicycle, which she's straddling, look rained-on.

"Who could've told you?" I ask.

"Missus Deaf," Mev says, turning her face to the figure in the plastic poncho seated out there on the bench.

"Come in," I say, throwing the door open. "Just wheel your bike into the kitchen and I'll towel it off."

"Where is she?" asks Mev, meaning the cat.

"Up there. Sulking. Still sitting in the bathtub."

"I'm ripping drain all over your carpet," says Mev.

"Well, that's to be expected, honey," I say.

399

Paulie and Mev are half-brother and -sister in that they both have me for a mom. Mev's dad is a Latin professor she doesn't see often but he's someone she likes. *I like him and I'm sorry for what all went wrong.*

I don't know about now but back then he was tall and his walk was slow and purposeful, one leg at a time, as if he were on stilts.

400

Whereas Paulie's father, who was never my husband, died years ago of a crystal-meth overdose. His sister Donna phoned me with the news and I told her, "That's too bad, Donna, I hope he went in peace."

"Well, again, it was crystal *meth,*" she said.

401

"I give fucking *up,*" says Mev, descending from upstairs, where she's been trying to coax the cat out of the tub.

Mev is shoeless now and showing the interesting Bugs and Daffy tattoo on the top of her bare foot.

"Mother, my God," she says, "for a woman who claims to have politics. You use mouthwash that's made by Dow. Scope, you should buy. Those people are saints."

I say, "You're so almost perfectly lucid on occasion."

We sit down in the living room. I offer her a candy slice.

I say, "I thought of another little piece of parental advice. A suggestion. Whenever I'm cleaning or have some task, when I'm almost at halfway, but don't want to think, guhg, I'm not even *half* through, I say, 'There, pretty much done!' and put all tools and equipment away."

"What does that do?" she asks.

"I don't know. It feels more...positive."

Mev's head is bobbing. She gives a little shrug. "I'll *try* it," she says.

She says, "That cat's like, suicidal."

402

My second ex complained to everyone about me, "She would've taken the washer and dryer if they weren't bolted to a wall!"

I would say to that ex, "Let's try and see if we can't remember better, bitch. There was no washer. Now, was there. No dryer. Whatsoever. You didn't, in truth, own a bar of soap."

Where Are You Taking Me

They like me on the interstate, some of them. Not these drivers.

404

On the street here, it smells of bitter coffee, oranges, and the powdered sugar they put on everything. It smells of sex, bread pudding, of the river and the sea.

A Few New Dents in the Fender

All night long, Dix has been pestering me. Until I surrendered, crawled out of bed in the dark and came to sit way over here. I've lit two cigarettes, both for me. "Friend," I say, "it seems that my sleep is keeping you awake."

"I just wanted to hug you!"

That is *not* true. I say, "You skinny cracker fuck."

I say, "Permission, Dix. Like in school, when they gave you a hall pass."

He's nodding, saying, "Agree with you, honey. I can abide that," but speaking to there and there, because his vision is such and I've got the two smokes so he's telling both of me.

"Dix, Dix, Dix," I say. "Touch me again and I'll cut you."

"NO MONEY DOWN," says he.

406

It spooks me to look at the guy. Even now he is elegant and graceful, tall, and with dark, sweet-smelling hair. Put him in any jacket, any pair of jeans. One time he wore a *scarf.*

407

He left the TV blathering away, out in the living room, and from there its voice is yelling, "Actually, it holds a few cups! So you can stand at the ironing board for *several hours* and not have to refill."

408

We walk to an all-night bar on Julia Street near where he lives. He sits in the booth with his legs outstretched and gazes at the toes of his shoes, which he's patting softly together.

"I'll be WATCHING MY MONEY," he says as I make off for the restroom. Now some of the patrons are looking at me strange. The tile floor in here is a blinking checkerboard. The room's crowded, shoulder to shoulder. The stalls, all in use, have hand-painted shrieking-pink doors. Over the sinks, a girl grips and fires an aerosol can.

I have to remember to tell Dix, who's only used to talking to women in bars, that some phrases, "Angel Tits," for example, should seldom be used.

I have to remember to tell him, more generally, that I'm sorry and it's not working out.

Why Stir Things Up

"I'm a friend of your father's," says the voice of a caller.

"That surprises me," I say, fooling around. "I thought we were all still mad at him for leaving Mom."

"I don't know about it. I don't know your mother."

"That explains that," I say.

"Are you really Dilbert's daughter? Have I got the right person?"

"Two different questions," I say.

The man says, "I must've dialed wrong."

"No, it's me, I'm sorry," I say. "How may I be of help?"

"Well, the first thing you can tell me is what hospital."

"For my dad?"

"Yes, his leg's broke."

"It is? How do you know?"

"Ma'am, I come over this morning to deliver a pork roast. For which he already paid. And I find him lying out in his rose bushes unconscious with his leg broke. Both the dogs sitting there with him all night."

"How do you know that?" I ask.

He says, "Ma'am, I know the dogs."

410

The phone's ringing again. I say to myself, "Out of the way, that's for me!"

Still Feels Like Something's Missing

"What is it you're doing?" I ask, crabbing at Mev.

"Looking through the trash at all this stuff you shouldn't have thrown away. Holy kill-oh-lee, Mother, this is Grandma's good pie tin or something."

"Actually, it's not. Not Grandma's and it's a stove burner. And, Mev, that's not your cigarette," I say. "That's one you stubbed out earlier. Your present cigarette that you shouldn't be smoking is this one here burning the table edge."

I say, "I have to go see my father in the hospital."

"Nice way to tell me he's sick," says Mev.

412

I'm trying to get some travel clothes pressed in a hurry.

"Oh, that's not good," I say. "Getting spray starch all over the animal."

Just Try to Hold It Steady

I've stopped for the night, still one or two indistinguishable states away from my dad.

414

There's a lot you can do with paper and scissors, if you have scissors.

I don't, and I don't really look nice enough to step outside and walk across the gravel courtyard to the office of this motor inn to borrow a pair.

But there's a lot you can do with just paper. Folding it dozens of ways.

And trick yourself out of thinking about anything over at the side of your mind, all the stuff that's there throbbing, or whimpering, whichever's worse.

415

Television, television! I'll watch *Remington Steele* if it comes on. I'll watch *Matlock*.

416

Nothing very bad is going to happen. I see that now. They're selling Thom McCann shoes. Here's an Eyewitness News Team.

417

Now, my dad, he really has and owns nothing. I bought him a few things, essentials, and I've brought those to the Allegheny Convalescent Hospital.

What sickens me is that I shopped smartly for these items. I got the very, very best buys. Which I hadn't realized until now, as my father holds up the top to the blue pajamas that should be cotton.

418

His hospital room's the usual with a thick swinging door, gray floor tiles, white curtains with a stencil pattern, a chair, his bed, the air-temperature-control unit I am perched upon.

To kill the time, I pose a question. I ask my dad what he did during the war.

He says he was an engineer for the U.S. Navy.

And this was a good, fine idea, my asking. He tells me about sonar and reverb and heat search and echo. For eighty minutes, he's answering, telling me what he did.

I wish things were different and not going to end soon. I wish we were all of us younger and could go back.

He says, "Think of the sound that helicopter blades make on deep water—fwumph-fwumph, fwumph-fwumph."

A World of Love

Southern men are working in the southern heat—prisoners in lime-and-white-striped pants; bike cops in jackboots; a man with dreadlocks collecting cans; another wearing cherry-red scrubs who's pedaling a decrepit bicycle.

On and On and On

Busy at the computer, I say, "That noise has been going on and *on*. It is so distracting."

I say, "CAT WITH ITS HEAD TRAPPED IN THE BASKET HANDLE!"

421

"It is in fact an American stadium chair," says the television. "They were popularly covered with red vinyl."

Go Someplace

Three eleven-year-olds who live on my street lope over to the car while I'm at a red. They say, "*We* want to hear Al Green," and climb into the back of my car. The four of us ride happily around for a time. The sky has sunset clouds edged in copper.

"Drive us to Mr. Finley's," they say.

"This is right," they say as we bound along on a ruined street and on into a contemptible Southern slum where there are catfish hovels, hair shacks, weed plots, spiked wire fencing, a barbecue shed guarded by a sad, heat-soured dog. We pass a bar beaten to splinters and chips and a chalky, sun-bleached sign that once read "Fern's." There's shattered glass everywhere. I slow when they tell me, at the road's end, and drive onto the swollen and torn blacktop lot for Mr. Finley's, where plates of old pavement joggle the car and bounce us in our seats. The place is a one-window wooden box with video games, maybe frozen pizza.

I say, "You're not getting out here. I wouldn't get out here, so no one I know can get out here neither."

"We come here all the time," they say.

"That may be," I say, jerking the car into reverse, "but today you have to go someplace nicer."

"Wah, wah," they say.

But I shake my head, saying, "Isn't that too damn bad."

These Yellow Lights Must Mean Step on It

The laundromat's dollar changer is busted again and a woman asks if I have extra quarters.

I do. Dix took me to the casino last evening, where I won great buckets of quarters on a Wild Cherry slot machine.

This is a teeny-tiny woman asking. Who seems about to fade. With the machines turning in here, the heat is unbreathable. And whereas I'm slickered with sweat, this woman's skin has a disturbing matte finish.

I hand her nine dollars' worth of quarters and she hands me a sack of nine hundred pennies. I needn't count them, I'm certain they're all there.

424

The laundromat's rusty old soda dispenser gives me a plastic bottle of something carbonated and indelible brown, which I am taking outside now because in here, by being in here, I feel like I'm hurrying people.

"We're drying!" a married couple assures me, and I say to myself, "See, that's just what I mean."

425

This guy, however, I can take a lot out on. Always loitering here, sitting aboard the machines, talking embarrassing filth or carrying on and lying about serving in Nam.

"Come with me," I say and because he thinks we're going on an attractive date, he does.

Outside, I say, "We don't smoke in there. It bothers people."

"You're telling me what to do?"

"If it sounds that way," I say, "let it."

That Was Connie Stevens Wasn't It Handing out Samples of Cranberry Bread

Hollis and the Deaf Lady arrive to help me with the Bigfoot script. Both have said they're brimming with ideas. Hollis brings along a pencil and a legal tablet snapped to the clipboard he uses for Driver's Ed.

I put us in the breakfast nook so we can have the table and where there are enough seats.

"Yes, this is perfect for me," says the Deaf Lady, climbing aboard the padded bar stool. She leans this way and that trying to get comfortable, cocks the wooden heels of her shoes on the stool's lower rung. She smooths the fabric of her paisley skirt on her thighs.

"We don't have to do this. We could do something else, if you'd rather," I say.

"Do you have anything to eat? Do you have any raisin toast?" she asks.

"No raisin," I say.

I open the refrigerator and stare at the contents, stoop and consider what's positioned toward the back. "Does...either carrot, or pineapple juice sound good to you? Or I have this pint of Ben and Jerry's that's almost soft."

Hollis says to me over his shoulder, "You see that small door at the top there? It leads to a compartment where you can keep foods extra cold."

"Is that chicken?" asks the Deaf Lady, peering around me.

"Yesterday's," I tell her.

She says, "No."

"In a *suit*, yet," she says to Hollis. He's wearing an inexpensive navy-blue suit.

"Yes," he says, "I had to work this morning. I'm a member of the working force."

"I used to be," she says wistfully.

"You were?" I ask as I'm sitting down. "What part?"

"Wildlife," she says. "Well, so to speak. It was really more like forestry, up in the tall trees."

"Lord!" I say.

"And a lion tamer some nights when I finished designing sweaters for the Gap. Could I have a different chair, please?"

"Certainly may," says Hollis. He gets off his and scoots it over for the Deaf Lady. "Work can be gratifying," he says, hoisting her bar stool over her and into place. "It's good to be good at something."

"Hmm," I say. "Yes, I suppose. I'm a pretty fair gardener. An excellent driver. I was a good pet owner until that went out the window."

"You were never a good pet owner," the Deaf Lady says.

"What do you mean? I was so. What did I do incorrectly?"

"Fed it junk food," she says and nods on the word for emphasis.

"I never. Did not. That is completely false."

"Cool out," she says. "Christ. I'm just expressing an opinion."

"You're entitled," Hollis says.

I say, "I just wish it were a right one. Or an opinion based on fact."

"All right, listen, folks," the Deaf Lady says, smiling. "I don't want to do this if you're just going to squabble."

"You're right. So right. Beg your pardon," I say.

Because I notice she put *makeup* on for this and Hollis has that fresh tablet and his sharpened pencil on the tabletop.

"Bigfoot's played by a guy in a suit of fur? Or special effects, or what?" asks Hollis.

I say, "They don't tell me. That's in a whole other department. I just deal with the writing. Period. Yeah, a human actor will be under there probably."

"Then...would this be a Caucasian gentleman in the role?"

"She doesn't follow you," the Deaf Lady says. "Or see the difference."

I say, "What is the difference?"

The Deaf Lady puts her elbows on the table and hunches down to look at me. "Bigfoot could seem symbolic to some people."

"Symbolic of...?"

"The big black bogeyman hiding in the bushes."

"First of all, nonsense," I say.

"Maybe to you," says the Deaf Lady.

"Second," I say, "and you'll be able to believe me on this: Nobody anywhere near this script is that clever."

"Let's just go on," Hollis tells us.

He says, "Here's what I've got so far." He's folded back the top sheets on his tablet to reveal a page of handwritten notes. He reads, "First off, I think there should be several realistic chase scenes, and then there should be spliced in a lot of newsreel-type footage, you know? Like with the Chinese capturing Bigfoot. Next, maybe take out the dairy farm." He looks up at us. "I've seen that one before." He looks back at his notes. "Then, you show your Justine character being a little selfish. A birthday party, is what I scribbled down. Followed by a department store where she exchanges and returns all the gifts. Also, I think she should have a cell phone. Then, I think get rid of the scene where her former boyfriend gets mistaken for a demon and beat up and thrown in a ditch. 'Cause it didn't really seem like he deserved it, but whatever. *Substitute* a scene where he appears at her door *already* beat up by somebody. Then, have Bigfoot gathering up to seek revenge, and walking out, he says, 'I am too old for this shit.'"

The Deaf Lady and I are both sitting here, nodding.

Hollis says, "Or another thing that could be possible is, give Bigfoot a sidekick."

427

The phone interrupts us and it's Dix calling.

He says, "Honey, Daisy's here with me and we been goin' over some of the problems. She's that psychic, in case you forgot."

"I can't talk right now," I say.

"Just try listening to her for two seconds. You don't even have to—"

"I would, but I really can't right now."

"She already knows stuff about the future, honey. She can *help* you."

"Hmm," I say, "probably not."

"You won't even *try* it? I can't *believe* you. You don't even wanna know if your kid has AIDS?"

"Unhh," I say.

I say, "Maybe some other time," and a new voice says, "This is Madam Daisy," just as I'm closing the phone.

Chapter Twelve

428

It's two in the morning. I'm miles from anybody, lost in Some-where, Louisiana. It's starting to thunder. I have my chest against the steering wheel and my neck stretched, trying to see. One finger's bleeding a trickle from where I cut it on the hinge of the pet carrier there in back. "This seems a lot worse than it is," I tell the cat. "Or your guess is a little off and it's worse than it seems."

I've driven down around a hairpin bend and into a canyon with a wavy line of oily black river and descending the hill there ahead are a half-dozen whipping snatching willow trees, coming for me and the cat.

429

I can't find a way to turn over certain playing cards, or to know which ones Paulie has seen.

430

"Please don't draw on me," Hollis says.
  I say, "I wasn't."
  "No, only your *hand* was."
  "You're such a five-year-old," I say. "I was discouraging, with my pen, the mosquito that just bit a hole in you."
  He looks at me, shrugs, looks again with a little smile. "This is...like you're going on a hayride," he says about my clothes. "It's cool, it's a kind of...inbred look. I mean, I like it. It's very ...Dogpatch."
  I stomp back up to the bedroom to take off the plaid.

Call Us with the Answer

The landlord stops by to say he's sold the place to a new owner.
  "Sorry to see you go," I say.
  His head bobs, thanking me. He says, "That must be your daughter that I've noticed coming around."
  "Probably is. The redhead?"
  "Whorehouse red," he says, as he plucks up a plastic bag that's blown onto the porch. "Always acts kind of flaky." He's squeezing the bag, making it pop.
  "Please," I say.
  "What? I didn't mean nothing."

I'm backing up behind the screen. "Why would you think it O.K. to insult my kid?"

"Lady...," he says, and pitches the wad of plastic into the yard. "You got a PMS problem. I didn't say a blasted *thing*."

"I just don't need to hear your remarks, whoever you are."

"Well, Miss Hoyt Tee Toyt."

"Is who *I* am," I say.

432

But I have a vivid picture of myself in a few short years—with a silvery bubble haircut, legs like a chicken's, baby-doll pajamas, hiding in some room, singing along with James Brown.

433

It's a mistake when Mev's Flub-a-Dub routine obscures the deeper layers of her person.

434

So plants, I guess, *like* smoke?

Keeping Sight of Your Goals

Most of the men from the weight room at the gym have asked me out. It's always six in the A.M. when I go and the men at that hour are ninety-nine years old, they have minutes left to live, they're alcoholics. They would ask me if I were a button or a stick. They would say, "Want to go for drinks?" and ask if I'd drive them to the carryout.

436

"I'm sure," says the Shoney's diner behind me, "that some Europeans have problems."

Where Are You Taking Me

Months ago, after Hollis was house-sitting here, he left his dopkit and possessions out on the vanity in the washroom. Mostly what he had there was poor-guy crap. I did notice he owns a Mason Pearson hairbrush.

"If you like that so much I'll buy one for you," he said.

And a little while later, he said, "Still mean to buy you that brush."

438

Here I am. Holding an orange strip of ribbon and a sheaf of gold foil paper, folded by a person who has not wrapped many gifts and tucked around this genuine Mason Pearson hairbrush that Hollis left on the front steps as a surprise for me today.

On the handle right where my thumb touches, there's a pinhead chip in the wood. I noticed this chip on the handle months ago. I am noticing it now.

These Are the Odds and Ends

"I don't mean to be rude to you," I say into the phone. It's ten-thirty at night and the prosecuting attorney is at her desk.

"You can't help it," she says quickly.

"Maybe you don't know exactly who you're dealing with, not how that sounds. But, have you had a hard look at Paulie? The plan is for him to participate in a trial?

"If I have to I'll subpoena him," she says, "to testify."

"Or," I say, "to march into court and build a refrigerator, which he could just as soon do."

"I really don't mean to be so rude," I say.

440

I call her back, crying this time. "Garnet," I say, because that is her name, "did you know he was a lacrosse player? Or that he turned down scholarships so he could live in New York? Zoology is his major. He's interested in the ram."

"I'm a mother too," she says.

I say, "I mean rams who are animals with horns, not the constellation."

I say, "I don't want you thinking he's just a goddamned little fruit."

There's More

Paulie and Armando are like some old couple who communicate with each other invisibly.

They had been playing poker when I was there and I watched and both of them were cheating.

They made a pot of cocoa and smoked cigar-sized joints and sat out on the balcony cackling, and ignoring me, because they were trying to have their lives.

Here Are My Questions for Today

I sit myself down and say to myself, "I'll just hurry ahead and get this over with:

"Where's the phone book?

"Is this the last coffee filter?

"Car's in the front or the back?

"Wait, was that a wreck?

"Who let this moth inside?

"How? By causing everybody pain?

"Did I already take this, or was that yesterday?

"Isn't that the same woman collecting for the March of Dimes?

"Where's the rest of the Frosted Flakes?

"What pickup truck? What landfill project?

"Where's the screws that came with this?

"Isn't that, I mean, way too tight?

"Who else is going to be there?

"O.K. if I just pay half?

"Who tied this in knots?

"You mean Aunt Jemima is really a person?

"All right, *what*?

"Whose handprint is this?

"The newspaper girl again? Did you not receive my check?

"How did this juice stain get here on the carpet?"

443

Some friends of Dix have dropped by so I'm moving over into the bedroom with my skeins of yarn or whatever these are. Earlier today I did decide I'd learn to knit.

444

I'm cross-legged on the bed, shoulders forward, working these two very long knitting needles.

This is a bedroom in which I have spent time but in the dark always.

There is a photograph of the parents, wealthy, still married, and with only Dix for a child.

Dix owns properties. He doesn't really work, or have much education, and his hobbies are going out and going out to clubs and standing in the center of the street in the French Quarter any night of the year and drinking his fill.

This room has yellow wallpaper with a rodeo cowboys pattern. There's a lamp whose base is a lucky clover.

"Man, we gotta get a drummer, that's all there is to it," says one of the guests out there.

"Yeah, shit," says another. "I've been thinking that same thing."

"Is this a money issue, Charlie, because that fuckin' sucks," says a third voice.

"I'm the drummer," Dix says.

"How're we supposed to advertise, let alone get any promotion, hopefully, in the future, when we're not a fuckin' band 'til we get somebody."

"I've always been the drummer," says Dix. "Been there, been the drummer."

"No, you know what we are?" someone asks. "Or what we friggin' look like we are? A coupla Teds."

There's snickering, shifting around. Maybe they're getting set to leave. I hear shoes scraping, hands slapping, mumbling, I hear the door.

"Dix, are you there?" I call out eventually. "Come on back to the bedroom and talk to me a second."

"About what?" he says, leaning in the doorway.

Here is a person who wishes he were dead.

I look up, frowning for him. "People think they're being clever sometimes and it's mean," I say.

"Could be right," he says. His hand goes to the doorframe and ticks at a splinter piece there.

But I'm not really his girlfriend and I shouldn't be commenting. And for kindness and comfort, he could find far better to turn to than me.

445

I'm at my desk, and, for his script suggestions, writing out a pretty hefty check to Hollis Tarryton Lamar.

Wad Up the Instructions and Just Figure It Out

Standing in the shower, just after I've stopped the spray, I hear a sound like a torturing psychopath crawling along the little hallway. I'm frozen here, naked and wet, waiting for the sound again or for nothing.

"And that," I get to say, "was just a sample."

What I need is something to fuss with and right here, *bath mats* lacking labels and mistakenly filed on the LMNOP shelf of the linen closet.

447

"Armando will be the best witness," says Garnet. "When I try to depose him he just *weeps*."

"Where can I be during the trial?" I ask.

"Uh, you should stay in the witness room with Paulie. Until it's time. And then an officer will escort you. We'll place you opposite the witness stand. That's also in view of the jury. So, it's all right to react? Nothing exaggerated. You'll keep it natural."

Get the Bugs off Me

I say to myself, "We got a new day. Let's just walk around the house and put shit where it goes."

A lot goes down the disposal after I've warned the cat, "Stand clear."

Batteries Running Low

"Wait, wait," Mev says as we're moving her bookshelf. "This has to wall against the up ago."

"They're your books," I say.

At the screen door is Sasha, Mev's birthday dinner date. He looks a little like Ross Perot. Which is a look that not everyone could carry off.

"Where'd you say you want this?" asks Hollis, walking bent over with Mev's green armchair balanced on his back.

She gestures at the screen door. Sasha lets himself inside.

"Same place as before the rug," she tells Hollis.

This red-and-rust-patterned Navajo rug is a birthday gift from me. I was in a trance for hours buying it—I went to several places, had trouble deciding, thought the rug was over-priced, wasn't sure Mev would like it, wasn't sure if it would go.

450

Now she and I are sharing the washroom, rinsing our hands, streaking on makeup.

"Will you please try to be nice to Sasha?" she asks me.

I lean into the wall mirror and, with my mouth opened slightly, stroke vitamin-E cream below my eyes. I say, "Well, but that usually comes off pretty much like it sounds. In my experience."

Mev cranks the hot-water faucet slowly on, and off, and on again. "He's someone else from the Methadone clinic."

"Ugh," I say.

"All right, then I don't want to do this," she says.

"No, *I* don't want to do this," I say. "This is like—"

"I know!"

"Like someone's—"

"I *know*," says Mev. Which is just as well.

She says, "Goddamn it, Mother. I wish you'd think of Methadone maintenance as a good thing. As therapeutic."

"Why do you wish that? It's not!"

Mev's glance in the mirror leaves me and she's off in thought. She's still facing the mirror but with her eyes locked. "I didn't set it up," says she.

451

Back in Mev's living room, Hollis is leaning off his seat on the sofa, unboxing the red fire extinguisher that is his birthday gift to Mev.

And if I'm not mistaken he's telling Mev's dinner date all about David and Goliath.

"No, it's different from what you heard," Hollis says. "It was for financial gain, is how it started, and to get his family exempt from taxation. But then there's weird parts, that're even gross. Like, King Saul starts fucking with him and says, fine, hotshot, then you bring me a hundred Philistine foreskins. So what's David do, brings him two hundred."

We're here, the three of us, standing silent and in a row.

"Well, lookit," Hollis says, a little flustered. "I can think this stuff or share some of it. You people choose."

Sometimes I Find My Place in Selves I Shouldn't Be

Mev is visiting, seated on the carpeting with her knees up and her feet planted and pointed out, today in a shirt that's stitched with the word "Tuna."

"What've we got here?" I ask, joining her on the floor.

She lifts the lids of her different metal tins for me, pokes into one and stirs the ingredients. "It's craft shit, Mom. Beads and the like.

"But I did wanna show you this from Grandma," she says, presenting a pretty blue envelope addressed in my mother's hand.

I say, "A card? Or, from my mom, I bet it's a card and a check."

"No, but a *fat*—yes, there's a card in there. But I mean, a disgracefully nice check. For no reason but a *birthday.*

"I'll pay her back!" Mev says, and sniffs and smooths tears away with her finger.

"Oh, sweetpea," I say.

I say, "One time, a while ago, I made up a thing to declare

about myself, and kept saying it, over and over. It went, 'I'm very lucky, I never get sick, I always—'"

"You *don't* ever get sick."

"I think this is why.

"Whereas you..."

"Listening," says Mev.

"Are surprised when somebody's good to you. Or you expect to fail at everything. You're always sure you're gonna get fired."

"I *do* get fired."

I say, "I think this is why."

But Now I Really Must Go

The Deaf Lady's standing at the sink, water running full blast and now the disposal. "No, I hear you," she says. "Get to the part where you run into your lookalike."

"Oh," I say. "Perhaps I've told this one before."

Chapter Thirteen

454

My flight to LA feels very downhill. There are a great, great many people from the South crammed into this plane. The overhead luggage compartments are bulging. My feet are trapped. There's nowhere to put my arms but crossed in front of me. In fact, *all* the passengers I see have their arms crossed in front of them.

Here come the attendants with a beverage cart they're forcing down the aisle. They'll be fatigued and debilitated and out of Diet Coke before they ever get to me. And why not put into service a cart that *fits?*

Movie People

Here's a tin of cookies Belinda sent over for me—hard and *sandy* with sugar. You could file your nails with these.

No Sloppy Seconds

Evan is about the same age as Dix—over thirty, under a hundred.

"I'm ignoring you," I say, but he climbs into bed with me, nonetheless.

I remember the last time we tried this. It was drudgery, a chore. In fact, Evan's interest in me has been a chore. Where his eyes follow me compulsively and he will exhaust himself complimenting me down to the buckles of my shoes.

I Think I Hear My Mom Calling Me

"This isn't good," I say beneath him.

I say, "Compared to almost anything. Compared to being at a company picnic, where we would, each of us, be having a better time."

"You mean if we," he says, "broke apart from the main group...."

458

"Hell," I say to Belinda. "I'm sure you have reasons for what you do."

"I have problems," she admits.

We're in the tea room in A Building, where the tables are covered with cloth and the baskets still have a few crackers.

Belinda wears a Burberry that's size Huge, that perhaps she borrowed from a bigger woman. A gray suit. The jacket's hankie pocket is defective and gaping and for that, I imagine, her browbeaten tailor was made to adjust his price. Dark red leather shoes I'll find fault with, given more time and a better view.

"What sort of problems? Like, from where they're repaving, you got tar on your car?"

She blinks, glances off.

"Or…," I say, "you missed a premiere. You're coming down with a cold—"

"Shut, up," she says to me.

She ate nothing. She trashed her dessert cake; knifed it to crumbs.

I ate even less, of my—bird skeletons, I think it was, under the aspic.

459

We'll sit here. I'll sit. I'll wait, and look like I'm just waiting and as though naturally what I prefer to do is be pinned here with no book and smokeless while I sit back and wait.

Let's Get This Over With

"So you're the South," says Hamfield, who lowered into Belinda's seat after she gave it up. He's bringing a sandwich from his knapsack, also a pint of Choco-Soy. We worked together over at Fox, he and I. Brandon Hamfield. His glasses are thick and his gaze is trading around behind them. He chews his nails. Otherwise, I'm content to talk to the man.

"No, my home's in the South," I say. "I don't represent it."

"What do you represent?" he asks, low, and now I remember why I detest men.

"You know they call me RM," he says, "for Rich and Mysterious."

Abhor, despise, and hate them.

Would Anyone Happen to Know

I find myself at the producers' meeting a minute early. In this long, anonymous room with its blinds and sisal matting. What is wrong with me? And I know that something is wrong because all the feeling just went out of my feet.

I Have a Little Diary, Too

The executives arrive at once, chuckling and chatting. They're groomed, blown, prepped, toned. They take seats in the high-backed chairs around the table. Belinda settles next to me.

And here's Penny, rolling a chair out, and sitting down across from us.

I'm watching as Belinda draws items from her tote bag—each item bearing the logo of a nightclub or salon.

I ask, "How did you get away with swiping all that stuff?"

"You said what?"

My hand is out, palm up, pointing. "All this great stuff that you filched."

Belinda is horrified that I've spoken to her this way. And why don't I learn? Penny winces, drives a hand through his hair.

"I too," I say in an effort to repair, "am the same way. I regularly see things I want to steal."

"Don't purshue this," says Penny.

I can't stop. I say, "Out in Fairbanks, those signs that read, 'No Shooting from the Highway.' Now those, I wanted to steal."

"Yeah, the shines," Penny says, irritated.

"But they were all shot up," I say.

He says, "Exshackly!"

463

I'm in the Chateau Marmont, for the moment. And that is the Belushi Death Suite in there. I recognize it from *Wired*. Penny's here and I'm asking him to tell me honestly what's happening to my mind. "It's going," he says, eyebrows raised.

464

Whatever the impression I gave, my confession was about *temptation*. Places I go, things I see, I have the urge to just take them.

Who Are You, Really

Evan's back living with his wife. Which I'm anticipating he'll mention. I can wait days, though. Nothing else but work to do.

He walks over here, now over there, his hands folded and pressed to his mouth.

"Squirrels," I say.

He says, "Interesting."

"Caused the calcium to drain from my body."

I bet I could say things about kerosene and wire cutters and Evan'd keep nodding like that.

466

What it takes to survive out here is *order*, I realize and say to myself, "Divide the day into equal periods. See this travel alarm? You get up, don your uniform, move according to the bell."

467

I'm wondering—in this restaurant with sidewalk seats and yellow sun umbrellas, terra-cotta floor tiles, a wait staff in blue-and-white seersucker—how old could the couple behind me *be?* "We can't do that drive at our age," they say. "Or even sit, for any period of time, not with our backs."

Just Came to Watch

Here's a man in his forties, with a sideways smile, in black-and-white bartender's clothes under a red satin vest.

Coming along after him, a fellow with an anxious face. He wears baggy fatigues and a John Lennon T-shirt.

Over there is a foolish-looking motel, its long porch lined with metal rockers that have never been and will never be rocked in.

There, a parked station wagon filled with newspapers and beside it, a woman in a tight-cinched apron, making change.

Sorry I Said Anything

Armando is Portuguese. He works for a jeweler, I believe, repairing watches and clocks. He wears polo shirts, usually, cardigans, leather moccasins.

I called him earlier this evening, and talked to him at his place of work.

He said, "Pleece, Mrs. Bread-on, don't bide *my* head off."

He said, "I only specked to him on the phone too. Heat's not like aim standing there."

470

"I was a moron. That's all they'll talk about in court. How it was my own fault," Paulie tells me.

I say, "I don't really think that would work as a defense."

"Why not, if it's true? I let the guy in!"

"Because—"

He says, "You're just ignoring the parts here you don't like."

He says, "All I thought was, he was nicely dressed. He looked like a businessman. He needed a restroom. And there is *nothing*, if you knew the area, *nothing anywhere* on Cowley or on St. Croix."

I say, "Paulie, if you can hear me."

"No, you may *believe* there's someplace, but there isn't."

"I don't care," I say. "None of this. It doesn't matter. You let him in, you married him, gave him sandwiches, I don't care. He still! Does not get! To hurt you!"

"The week before," says Paulie, "I saw a guy trying to defecate into a paper sack."

471

Yes, and down there is Sunset Boulevard, and no, I don't care about that either.

472

I've kept my cab waiting. The driver's out of patience. "You the right one or not?" he calls when I appear.

I hold him up even longer, trying to answer.

"Just get in, get in," he says. "Where you going?"

"I'll tell you in a minute," I say.

After exactly a minute, he says, "You decide yet?"

He looks around at me. "No," he answers for himself. "You don't wanna go nowhere?"

He pulls over, counts to three, pulls out. "Then it's back to where you came from."

I don't argue.

He peers at me in the rearview. "What've you got?" he asks. "Man trouble?"

"My son," I say, ashamed of myself before it's out of my mouth.

Could Stand Here for Hours

Belinda is hurriedly destroying the three-page outline I wrote this morning—crumpling it, tearing it, batting the papers into the trash.

She's a small woman, clear-eyed, an equestrian in her free time, very blond, teeth the size and whiteness of Chiclets.

Her chair's a little high for her, I notice. Her pale blue pumps are an inch off the floor. She speaks with her neck arched forward, her jaw flexed.

"Listen to me carefully. When I tell people they've made mistakes with a script, they make every effort to do *better*. You can decide about that for yourself, but your attitude—don't interrupt me. I'm perfectly right to speak."

With both hands she grips the edge of her desk. She says, "This is demoralizing. Have you thought about that? It makes what I'm trying to do impossible."

On a tray near the door here is the Hawaiian fruit platter Belinda had for lunch—twizzled citrus rinds, a scraped melon hull, a teensy vine plucked of all but a few grapes.

Her blue pumps have stopped moving. She sits now with her hands clutched tightly. "It makes me crimson with rage to have to submit this revision. If we had another day, by damn, I *wouldn't*. With this newsreel *preposterousness,* and these Chinese. I *deleted* that demon character, yet here he is again. Bombing raids on the phone company? I can't *imagine* what the studio's response will be. I only regret it reflects on me. You don't see this, do you? No, I thought not."

I'm leaning in a little, my shoulder on the doorframe. I say to Belinda, "Bite! Me! *Farm*-girl!"

474

I'm out of here, at any rate. Before she can pull a gun. I'm old, can't think, can't know this individual.

475

This now is just a bit of arithmetic for me: If coffee has six percent caffeine and decaf is ninety-seven percent caffeine-free, it's got half.

I just can't decide if I *want* coffee or anything—a tranquilizer? A soft drink? Would I like to hear music on the radio? Or should I get out the travel iron and do the collars on my shirts? I can't decide. There's some dark metallic something razoring around in my chest.

476

One thing is certain and that's that I need a shoeshine. For this next part, my shoes should not be scuffed.

Where, in this bungalow, is the appropriate place for a shoeshine? I've swabbed liquid polish all over and now I must stand here with my feet on this newspaper from now on. I could have just instructed people, "Don't look at my shoes."

477

Penny phones my room at this late hour. "Show...," he says. "What's shup?"

I'm not telling him about the shoeshine mess or that I also polished my wallet.

It's Not What You Asked For

In my notebook I've scribbled a list of all those who were ever kind to me. The list is about the same length as a list of those who weren't. Some folks should have been nicer. However, some of the good folks on List One were also in error.

479

"I need you to tell me something," I say to Garnet over the phone. "What do you think, if Paulie does this, will be the out-come?"

"Attica," she says.

"For?"

"About fifty years."

"How would you manage *that*?"
"The photographs."
"Of what?" I ask.
She says, "They're of Paulie."

480

And now my suitcase should be loaded for home—recorder,
bathrobe, Sweet 'n Low, stockings, mouthwash, flashlight,
suits, underwear, string, three bottles of Visine.

Letter to Sean Penn

I write:

> You should be allowed to punch any kind of photographer
> you want. I think.

Mrs. Sean Penn

P.S. You've made films about everything and been in them.
Maybe *you* know why some freak would do heinous shit to
my kid.

Hate to Keep Asking

I slept a couple hours, woke up and gazed around the room;
heard nothing, saw nothing. Slept another hour. Awoke rolled
up like a *creamhorn* in the bed comforter, and had to rock back
and forth to get free.
There. Now I can lie here.

483

Penny's lingering with me while I diddle around this complicated seven-foot vending machine. "At least it takes dollars," I say for something to say.

He's wearing a yellow windbreaker today, with his gray trousers and espadrilles.

I don't know how my own tired mouth can keep on working so tiresomely. "You like it O.K. at Mercury Brothers?" I ask.

Penny's mouth makes the slightest pout and he shrugs. "Sometimes," he says.

"Do you live, where? In the city?"

"No, a little ways out," he says.

I now have a knee and a shoulder pressed against the vending machine. I'm shoving dimes and quarters into the coin slot and squashing the change return button at all about the same time.

Penny can guess, surely, waiting behind me, that I'm just here doing this.

Leave Some for Others

My mother declares something when I phone her from the hotel. I have my butt on the side of the elaborate bed, my legs stretched out and my feet pointing. She says she's packing it up and moving to Whozitville to take care of my father.

"That *is* crazy," I say

"Well, how would you prefer it?" my mother asks.

I'm staring at my legs in their stockings. "That Dad could hire nurses if he had a nickel to his name."

And now I'm bawling and saying, "I feel horrible, horrible. These are *nineteen-dollar nylons* I have on today."

"Well," says my mother, "Right there! That's money you could have sent to your dad."

485

This bathroom is small, white, equipped with a clear shower curtain, paper-wrapped soaps, stacks of towels, mats and wash-cloths on a wire shelf, samples of green hair products good on any kind of hair.

I'm at the mirror, wondering, for being alone in this bunga-low, how contoured with blush powder need my face be?

I tarry in here, thinking about this strange life. The little coffeemaker on the counter signals every eight seconds with a "snick."

Now smoking with my back to the mirror. Next at the opened window. There's a half-moon out there, and below people hurrying from the front lobby and in their weird clothes, bustling off. They're like someone talking delightedly about something you'd reject! And there's what I can't see—a freight train skidding twenty feet, an air-conditioning unit gar-gling. There's a janitorial staff, somewhere above me, working with a furious carpet steamer.

486

"Is 'annoyedly' a word?" I ask myself.

"No, I don't think so," I say, shaking my head.

487

If I could take a break from work I could read all my books, contact everyone, clean everything, learn to play the drums, drive to Quebec, Canada, and I would try to come back right away.

And What Did You Learn

I write on a postcard:

Dear Dad,
Be nice to my mother.

Mrs. Sean Penn

489

I cross out everything except the "Dear Dad" and write:

I miss you so much.

490

With Belinda in her office at Mercury Brothers. I'm to sit quiet while she studies the executive producers' memo. My God, this is so unpleasant! Time is at almost a halt. Interns have been trundling the same piece of equipment down the corridor. The coffee percolator has been popping on and on. That guy, for hours, has been maneuvering to park his vehicle.

Belinda raps the desktop twice as she finishes reading the memo, shifts back a little in her chair and turns to me. She fingers the cultured pearl in her earlobe. She says something inaudible, maybe "I forgot to swim today," picks up her pen and writes "pool" on a pad stolen from the Beverly Wilshire Hotel.

So I give up. Yes, I am stupid. I just start saying anything— weather/ballgame/read your horoscope/cowlneck/car mileage things about no one, for no one. Lint, really, from my mouth into the air.

Belinda stops me with a wave finally. She says, "Well, I never. They've *accepted* the revision and they offer their full support. Meaning, we've ascended to the next level and can start the final wee-reet. I mean, rill-wite...rear-while. Ridiculous! Why can't I sree that rurd?"

491

Maybe it's *me*.

Simple Machines

"You've got them in the car...," Penny says, with his laptop up and ready to go.

"In the car," I say.

He says, "So, now they're driving..."

"The car's...green," he says, typing in "green."

He says, "Green car. They're in it..."

I rub my right temple, a throbbing there. I say, "Wind. Snow. Car's green. Absolutely stuck. Justine gets out. Twists of exhaust. *Blinding* snow. Uses her shoulder, and tries to push. Way in the distance, we see a sandplow, just a tiny winking light—"

"The other extreme," Penny says.

"What?"

"A hundred degrees hot and it's dry."

"It's the Alaskan bush! We can see McKinley."

"So dry," he says, "you wouldn't dare light a match."

"I'm not doing this," I say, crossing my arms.

"Bigfoot's got a wooden matchstick between his teeth," Penny says. "And she warns him, 'It's so dry. You'd better not light that match.'"

"'You'd better not light that,'" he says, typing. "'It's so—'"
"This is crackball," I say.
"No...sit still," he says, reaching to pat my arm. "I was just following a thought. Sit still. It could be a nice moment, but forget it, forget it. We'll save only the matchstick and that's all. We can learn how dry it is later.'"

493

I must always remember that the best anything I could hope for is that this script passes muster, the movie gets made, and my jokes are made known to dumb white people.

494

I'm lollygagging in the cafeteria. At a table not so far behind a clutch of my colleagues in the biz. Ordinarily, I can't follow their industry yap or remember any of the people they're junking. Today's pick, however, is Belinda Juris-Janeway.

And I agree with every ugly word they're whispering. Up until this personal part about her knees and throat and weight and teeth and nose and eyebrows. Goddamn it, now I have to get up and go over there.

"Hey, people," I say. "The woman gives seventy percent of her income to the blind. This level y'all are focused on, this is not cool."

But now, walking off, I regret mixing in and making up lies. I never liked Belinda, I still don't. She probably was a tubbo. *Those* people, however, are like a jellied acid that adheres to you and sets you on fire and eats down through to your bones.

Ask to Speak to Whoever's In Charge

I know damn well Hollis is constantly at my place, that he's there copying documents, taking photographs and fiber samples. When I get him on the phone, he says, "Right, what else is there to do but rummage through your undie drawer?"

I say, "I want you to realize those aren't representative undies you're seeing there. I brought with me any that were any good."

496

I've tabulated the three things Hollis most often says to me. They are:

"You'll live."

"What don't you understand?"

And, "Fuckin' pick one or the other."

What Can I Do for You

Penny is seated with his palms on his knees. He'll move his hands to the chair arms in a minute and grip them as Belinda sharpens her tone. I'm wondering what drew him over from Paramount to work on a Bigfoot movie besides millions and millions and millions of dollars.

He breathes in, pulls himself up, and starts again: "Itsh dry cold. Killing cold. Fifty or shixty below sheero."

"And...how are we suggesting this?" asks Belinda.

Penny thinks a second. He says, "Bigfootsh noshe ish bleeding. Show Jushtine handsh him a Kleenexsh."

"My nose bled the whole time we were in Fairbanks," I say,

just so Penny can take a rest. "He's right. Dry cold, that is right."

Belinda looks at me and squints at me and wonders what I'm about.

She says, "Her hankie, rather. Let's go with that. It could be a nice moment between them."

No Strung-out Queens

We're hurrying out in the hallway at the same time, but I'm taller than Belinda and longer-legged and she can eat my dust.

Chapter Fourteen

499

Something is going on down there, below us in this airplane.
Like a game board—circles and squares, huge circles, huge
squares and hundreds of them. I will never know what that's
about. This now could be parquet flooring and here's all of a
sudden a city—its glass and metal glinting with sunfire. It's
New Orleans, looking like a brooch.

A World of Love

On the freeway, headed home, quite low on gas, riding behind
Cheech and Chong.

501

I need something to eat that's not poison. But I guess that, for most folks, goes without saying.

Empty Your Pockets

I'm watching Mev hoe. While I was gone she kept up my flower garden. It looks quite good, but Mev doesn't. She's been withdrawing from Methadone. She acts as though maybe her eyes are bothering her, and she looks ashen, and her skin looks doughy and damp.

"What did you *do?*" I ask.

"Gave them," she says, "just like steroids."

503

Dark of the night and I'm ignoring the lightning bug, way up there, winking at the center of the ceiling.

Next, the Lee Press-On Nails

I would say to all the ex-husbands, "I think, from now on, whenever there's a situation or a little discrepancy you don't want to explain, go ahead and lie."

I would say, "Go on, go your way, keep it moving."

505

"The best music I ever heard in my life," I tell Martin, who keeps the list of songs, "was in my parents' car on the AM radio. It was Little Stevie Wonder's 'Fingertips,' Part One. And then, Part Two made me even happier."

"I'll take it into consideration," says he.

506

The Deaf Lady's forgotten me entirely tonight. I can tell from her expression she doesn't have a clue. "You're not going anywhere until your closet is cleaned," she says.

"Fine with me," I say. "There're plenty of interesting things in my closet."

I've been trying to toss this afghan around her and over her shoulders, flinging it like a net.

She does seem to recognize Hollis, who's joining us here on the walk.

He says, "I have the answer, not to all of life's problems, but numerous ones. A *wagon*."

She folds her arms and puts her weight on one leg and, standing like that, bobs her head in agreement. There goes the afghan.

Still Something Missing

Mev is seated across from me. She looks painted by Degas tonight.

It is a goulash of feelings I have for her just now.

508

I say, "This is my last and final piece of advice. That I know from years and years of marriage to different pigboys."

"Let's have it," Mev says.
I say, "Picnic foods."

509

"Are you still so dull?" Jesus asked them.

—MATTHEW 15:16

A woman named Marla is determined to sleep here in the laundromat and she wishes the doors closed as it's foggy and damp outside. I gift her with a black cashmere sweater I have shrunk in the dryer. "Marla?" I lie, "I'm giving you this because it's nice."

The place is empty at this hour so we each have our own table to lounge upon.

Ah, but here's the fake Viet Nam vet intruding on our party, scrambling onto a table beside Marla and me.

"Like yer little halter top," he says in my direction.

I say, "Don't have an opinion about my halter top, please."

"It was a frickin' compliment!"

I say, "Still. I'm not available for all your remarks. Compliment me just as well by keeping quiet."

Marla scoots over and sits close and passes me her little bottle of bourbon. "Now," I say, with my back to the man, "let's just stay sitting up and drink like ladies."

Why Stir Things Up

"What is your *name*?" I ask the Deaf Lady.

"Mrs. Robert Sanobel," she says.

"Huh," I say. "Wouldn't have pegged you for a Robert."

511

"Hot! Danger! Red! Run!" I tell the cat, but that does nothing. I say, "Canister vacuum!" Yes and *now* you see her tail flying.

She's a rewarding cat to have, sometimes, in my view. A moment ago we were sharing a smoke—I was blowing it, she was catching. Or, so was the goal as far as I could interpret things.

Why Is Everybody Leaving

Here I am pictured sitting demurely on the couch, wearing a red dress, my hair long and dark. In the foreground on the floor, Bob Dylan.

513

"What do you think of these celebrity divorces?" asks the Deaf Lady, herself again, more or less.

"Not a thing," I say. I have a Bartlett pear here, streaming juice. I'm holding it away from my linen trousers.

I say, "And I've gotta say I'm surprised that *you* do."

She shrugs. "You've been divorced. Don't act too superior."

"Not acting superior," I say.

"On the same subject," she says, "let me ask you a question. Where do you go to meet good men who aren't going to cheat on you and who're ready to make a commitment?"

This pear's keeping my hands busy. Otherwise, I'd bam my head in response. I say, "Nowhere! Such men don't exist!"

"What about your Dix boyfriend? Doesn't he fit the criterion?"

That shuts me up.

Eventually, I say, "I should do another round of research before I give out that information."

And it's not eight seconds before the phone rings and there on that end is Dix, weeping. He's an idiot but a weeping idiot who loves me and so I can't hang up.

There Is No They

Hollis has accidentally let the cat escape, he informs me. "Look," he says, "this was her will against mine. She's been a deranged psychotic *pest* ever since you brained her with that walnut."

Mev says, "Maybe so, but she shouldn't be outdoors. There're bad, evil people in the alleyway sometimes."

"I'm guessing...," I say, "boys?"

Turn Off the Radio

There's some news stuff about the Rodent Slime Criminal that Paulie's forbidden to see. "We're keeping charge of the TV remote," a detective tells me me over the phone. "There'd be no point in it, but to scare him."

"I'll tell you one thing about your guy," the detective says. It's a second before I realize he means the Crawling Thing Criminal. "Most people commit the first little crime or two. It gives them a sense of confidence. Now they're trouble. Now they're gonna do some real damage. Whereupon, they do usually embark on a career of worse crimes. Sometimes going all the way up. *Your* guy," he says, "got started that way. The middle-of-the-way crimes, he skipped right past them."

516

Mev's gone off to read the news.

Left the Door Open, Lid Up, Cap Off

He's dead, is what it is. The Sadistic Insect Criminal. His body was found in the prison's laundry room, stuffed, and with his head crushed, into a clothes washer.

Oh, and I would think that ought to be that.

518

"We'd like for Paulie to chill a bit," says Garnet.

She means he must stay a little longer in the icy sewer that is New York.

519

"Nothing, I'm fine. You?" Paulie asks me. He says, "I am anxious to get back to my fish."

520

I've chosen now as the time to be sick in a bucket.

521

I do want to call someone and pass along this news. Who? Here for hours studying the listings in my phone and address book.

Already Had Them Laughing

On one of the last days I was there, Armando disappeared with Paulie into the bathroom and then the door opened and Paulie was wearing a derby hat and black jeans and a black turtleneck.

"We forgot *wide* face but that's yet to come," Armando said.

Paulie said, "So I won't have to answer all kinds of questions about the gloves."

"Right, right," I said. "You might get a different type of request, though. Do the box, do the escalator, do eating a banana."

Whatever You Do, Don't Let Go

Hollis is in a chair before the long window looking drowsy in pj's, rubber slippers, a robe of some fabric too stiff to be flannel. He sits with his hands on his knees, his eyes unblinking. On the table beside him is a breakfast mug of steaming water he's staining with a green teabag.

It isn't daylight yet.

I'm pressed against the screen door, looking out. I can see the moving shadow of somebody in my car.

It's Mev's shadow, seems like. I'm going barefooted across the lawn, jerk the door open and say, "I thought you went home on your bicycle!"

"And...what? You no longer think so?" she croaks.

"Mev, don't be exasperating. I had thought you rode home on your bike."

I crawl inside, sit in the passenger seat. She looks wretched.

She says, "Mom, there's something disgusting. I knew that guy. Who raped and tortured Paulie. I got introduced to him in New Orleans at something, some soiree. I remember it perfectly."

"No..."

"Yes. It was the guy. I did. I'm totally, without a doubt, certain.

I'm shaking my head.

"Mom!" she says.

"What?"

"I bet I told him about Paulie. Braggingly. And gave him the address."

She says, "I'm all right, just keep quiet. There're things I have to figure out."

"Mev," I say, "you obviously need rest and then you'll feel better—"

"No. I will not, Mother. I'll *feel*. Not worse. But not better."

524

"Probably I'll go away," she says. "I have some friends in the Nevada desert who want me to get involved in that—whatever the thing—Paulist Fathers' Project."

"That sounds O.K."

She says, "Maybe. Those fuckin' priests better not discriminate against thinking about me."

"Better not," I say. "It is one of the risks you run, as a woman. That it's hard sometimes to rise above."

Deal from the House, Don't Pay Rent

A Goodwill truck is in the driveway of Mev's house and a clip-art-looking man in a uniform is loading up quite a lot of stuff she's giving away.

She comes out now carrying a wind chime in each hand.

I've been parked here, about a block off. On the seat I have this Nine West shoebox stuffed full of cash money she might want. I'm insane.

I'm not going to mess with this, and so start up the car.

"Say good-bye, Mev," I say.

526

Hollis is on the bench in the yard. He says, "Well, congratulate me. I've decided to run for office."

"No fooling, wow. What office?"

"Just, for Transportation Secretary," he says.

"Well, what an idea. Can you win, do you think?"

"Not really," he says, firming up his lower lip. "We'll have to see. That's not why I'm doing it. I want the exposure, want to meet people, get used to seeing and being seen."

527

A little more waiting and then I'll get the phone call. Maybe in another four or five weeks after Paulie's six-months test. When he'll be able to say he's virus-free. Or I'll answer and he'll say just, "Mom."

528

I meet up with Hollis on my sun porch. He's got *Gray's Anatomy* opened on his lap and his arm is up as he examines the parts of his wrist and right hand.

"Were you always like this?" I ask him.

"Always." He nods. "What've you got there?" he asks me.

"Oh, a parting gift I'm making for Mev. It's a macramé... I don't know."

He squints and says, "You've got to budget your time on a thing like that. When hours become days? Now it's kind of a tangle, isn't it? The girl might hurt herself. Were *you* always—"

"From day one," I say.

529

I run into Claude and Early and the Zieter brothers.

To Claude I am two separate women. He tells me I must meet my twin! It's uncanny, he says. He says this twice. To me, when he's going into the video store, and to me, when he comes back out.

I'm in the lot all this time because I'm waiting for the shift to change in there so I can go inside and with the least amount of embarrassment rent *Purple Rain* yet again.

Right Where You Left It

"'It's the memory of?'" sings my shrink. "'The land I love?'"

"O.K., fine, got it," I say.

531

"I hate this," says Hollis, shaking his magazine. "See how this title tells you, 'Stock Up on These Five Foods and Never Go Hungry Again!' Only the list is like...anchovy past. *Sorghum.*"

"I read it," I say.

He's ripping the pages of the article out and crunching them singly into little wads. Now lining them up on the chair's arm.

"Listen to this latest idea," he says and turns his focus to me. "Suppose Bigfoot's outside, right?, and shooting baskets, except he's using a milk crate instead of a hoop."

"I'll propose it."

"Lie away," he says.

I was lying but I won't anymore. I say, "How I read the producers' memo, about what they think and their recommendations, is we could put in anything you want."

"If *that's* true," says Hollis.

"Well, not—" I say, but he's up and off, in search of paper and a writing instrument.

532

Ah, but here in the alleyway is Flower Girl, my cat, and somebody's made a mess of her.

533

It's quicker to drive on this concrete strip where there're no other cars in the way and it's cutting a big, big corner to go over the lawn of this hair salon. If she's cold, I would be fine in just my bra if she needs my shirt.

I don't know. I don't know at all. I'm just riding her around now. Dead little baby.

At a time that seems so unfair.

Give Me a Hit of That So I Can Keep Coughing

"Are you alone?" I ask myself.

"All alone," I say.

535

I would say to my cat, "There's no place very safe for any of us anymore."

I would say, "I'm obliged to you for bringing that home to me."

And say, "Nothing about you really irritated me at all."

536

Hey, Joe in the CD player and now most of the men of my town are following me. Although, according to the mirror, which does not lie, I look like a Smurf doll. So I'm wondering, and would like to know, *what* must life be like for young attractive women?

"Pay attention to the fucking sunset," I tell myself, but I've been out here too long, I can barely keep awake.

"My dear, my dear," I say, "it's getting kind of late."

So, go home, I guess. Some sleep wouldn't hurt.

Acknowledgments

The author is most grateful to the Corporation of Yaddo, to Michael Sundell, and to Candice Wait for their extraordinary generosity and support.

The author wishes also to thank Dawn Seferian and Andrew Wylie for their kindness and their grace.

And to these dear and true friends, Roger Angell, Rick Barthelme, Karen Crowley, Rie Fortenberry, Virginia Harabin, Bob Hester, Laura Lark, Mark La Rue, Rick Moody, and Maureen Murray, my thanks.